Damaged Beauty

Joey Superstar

Margaret Gardiner

Moon—Sherman Oaks, CA
Paperback ISBN: 979-8-9917517-0-4
Hardcover ISBN: 979-8-9917517-1-1
Library of Congress Control Number: 2024921619
Damaged Beauty: Joey Superstar
Author: Margaret Gardiner
Available formats: eBook | Paperback distribution | Hardcover editions

Published in the United States by New Book Authors Publishing

DEDICATION

To My Boys.

ACKNOWLEDGMENTS

Andre and Brandon. My Nel boys. Two peas in a pod. There when asked. Thank you. Anet Pienaar whose answer to every comment is, "I can help." Ton Vosloo for offering to enable my dream. Marian Miller whose enthusiasm made me a believer. Rolene Strauss & her husband, D'Niel Strauss, who offered introductions when I was lost. Lady Bird, aka Caroline. I appreciate your tart commentary, eagle eye and all-around-friendship. Especially grateful to you for the collective title: Damaged Beauty - so people can find the next two books. Damaged Beauty: The Corruption of Charlie Cross. Damaged Beauty: Tara Bean - Plastic Paradise. Sandy Bronkhorst for listening and asking to read it. Beverly. Hannah Hargrove PR, your words, "It's a really good book," gave me wings and your PR confidence made me a believer. 'Being there' always, with relevant insight and generous sharing, I was so lucky to find you. Johan Coetzee. Alishia van de Venter. Starburst Public Relations. I felt like I found a partner, South African expertise at its very best. Wind beneath my wings. Thanks team. Jodi Hockensmith. JH Public Relations. I felt I couldn't do this without you. Thank you. Oliver Tolentino for clothing me for decades in designer wear that boosts my confidence. I thank the moon especially. For the texture, magic and inspiration. The breeze for its caress. The light which makes me swoon. Bernard Jordaan for changing my life. My mum for instilling fight in her three girls. My dad who taught me to see beauty. Willem Botha for the back cover photo credit. South Africa. The people. Their support over the years swells my heart. I am awed by you. Finally, thank you to all the strangers whose random acts of kindness to me have left me in awe of humanity.

To anyone who has been there that I've not named, forgive me.

This is for all the people who have been made to feel less. Whose voice has been quashed. For the beauties who have been made to feel ugly so someone who is ugly inside, can feel better about themselves. This is for the broken. For the people who get up each day and try. Beauty is not about how you look, it's in each of us, all we have to do is open our hearts, give others grace, and give ourselves a break.

If you feel alone, unseen, suicidal, tell someone, call a helpline, love yourself enough to fight back and believe that you are enough as you are. We are all worthy of love and lovable.

TABLE OF CONTENTS

ABOUT THE AUTHOR

Margaret Gardiner was a cover girl in Paris at 16, Miss Universe at 18, and fashion editor of goldenglobes.com. She's worked with A-list actors from Angelina Jolie to Zendaya. She knows what it is like to be on the red carpet and in the spotlight, and what goes on behind the scenes.

Twice nominated for the ICG Publicists' International Media Award, as well as the 'National Arts and Entertainment Journalism Award' by The LA Press Club, Margaret's first Best Seller: 'Margaret Gardiner's Complete Health and Beauty Guide,' was followed by 'Margaret Gardiner Winning in Modelling and Beauty Competitions.' Margaret holds a Bachelor of Science degree in Psychology and her research had been published on gender inequality, unconscious bias and DEI for several publications.

Hosting duties include as a co-host of the *Miss Universe Pageant* and guest host on *Good Morning South Africa*. She has also hosted panels with influencers on mental health, A-list Stylists on fashion, and women in entertainment on inequity. She has organized virtual panels on DEI in LA and at The American Pavilion at the Cannes Film Festival. The LA-based journalist has also hosted and participated in podcasts.

Still active in the world of beauty, 2023 found Margaret guesting on Miss Universe which was Telemundo's No. 1 entertainment program that night in adults 18-49. For many years she coordinated red carpet fashion for Goldenglobes.com including for the Award Show, Golden Globes.

Margaret has directed, written, and edited segments for television magazine programs and has written for *Marie Claire, Mademoiselle,*

People Magazine, etc. Newspapers include *The Sunday Times, The Weekend Argus,* and *Rapport*. She continues to interview the 'who's-who' of entertainment and her video interviews can be found on YouTube: *MargaretGardinerUniverse.*

Margaret, whose first poetry was published as a 16-year-old, continues to be a sought-after 'cover girl.' Margaret has walked in, sat front row, and covered Paris Fashion Week and recently walked in LA Fashion Week for designer Oliver Tolentino.

'*Damaged Beauty: Joey Superstar*' is the first book in the 'Damaged Beauty' series about good girls who play nice, are under-estimated, get damaged, find their voice, and break the barriers to become who they really are.

For every would-be fashionista, influencer, or model, here's a peek behind the proscenium.

1

JOSAPHINA BRINKLEY - AKA - JOEY
CÔTE D'AZUR: 1985

They'd driven east along the Côte d'Azur, the endless sky above, the Mediterranean a dirty blue to her right. The villas packed together vibrant oranges and creamy whites, like too much acne on an overcrowded cheek. The light was lemon, and she was sour.

A headache had throbbed when Josaphina – Joey – had awoken in the subtle Seurat hues of Nice before sunlight drenched the landscape vividly. She was exposed, naked and thirsty, on the silk sheets. Mascara smudged like an owl. Lips stained for sex – undefiled. Not alone. While she'd slept, her husband had returned.

The night before had been a desperate evening of laughter without humor as destruction filled the air. She'd entered the private soiree after everyone was seated, like a queen taking her throne, upright, aware of the looks, accustomed to them, discounting them, waiting for his that never came. Her body was like a racehorse - fine-honed, glistening in the candlelight like a well-oiled sex toy, unused. They were buzzards, searching for fresh flesh to feast and satiate, to distract from their personal destruction. Old love is tired, and his was exhausted. She didn't know why.

It had been a long time since she'd had sex, and she needed it. Everything reminded her of the act he seemed to have forgotten how to perform, at least with her. She drank fast and with a purpose. She spoke rapidly to anyone who would listen, though he never did, her laughter a little too long and a little too loud.

Joey noticed the blonde on his right, flirting with furtive smiles and secret touches. The woman's hand had disappeared beneath the table some time ago. Joey's man had straightened, his lips open, and his eyes narrowed as his companion's arm jiggled in the nether world. She saw the change in him.

I'm not crazy

The words flashed like a neon sign on repeat in her head. She inserted another.

Escape!

Joey pushed back from the table and walked away from him. Maybe she could play his game? Maybe prompt him to react? Her hand trailed the fine fabric of shoulders until she felt the tightness of muscle beneath her fingertips and stopped. He was a friend of a friend of her husband's, with strong forearms. She let her palm crawl down the side of his face to his chin and pulled his head back. The people around him stopped talking. The woman to his right froze with her fork midway between plate and mouth, confusion on her face. The man looked at her. He was beautiful. Hooded eyes, emperor's nose, and a mouth that was made for sucking. Joey rounded him, cutting off the woman on his right. Joey brought her face close to his and whispered with her hand in his hair, "Would you love me tonight?"

His eyes took in her platinum hair, the mountain range cheekbones, the inflamed mouth, and he said so softly she strained to hear. "A woman like you should not have to beg."

"I know."

"Fix what is broken. Make your life right." His expression like a mother looking at her wayward child, with comprehension and compassion.

That hurt more than a blow, for it mirrored her desperation. She loped out onto the patio and down to the pebbled beach, slowing only to scoop up an open bottle on her way to the shore. She sat alone and drank as the clouds cruised the sky, and the sea made soft laughing sounds. Then she lay back in the sand, looked at the black heavens, and dreamed that her man still cared.

She awoke chilled, the beach ingrained on her soft parts, sandpaper rough, like her heart, scratched and scarred. The wind had picked up while she slept, a cloying minstrel wind that felt like a thousand caressing strokes. She arched at the pleasure and pretended it was her husband's touch. The pretense pained. The lack of physical contact had been too long. She retraced her steps through the floodlit garden, ignoring the fuchsia and succulents. Beauty was nothing; it was no balm to her yearning. Joey climbed the flat stairs to the patio, peering into the private room. It was deserted.

Heels in hands, she by-passed the table still baring remnants of the repast, like a talisman to what had been, and what no longer was. Joey climbed the stairs to their quarters. She opened their door. The room was empty, like her womb.

If she'd been able to carry the fetus to term, would he be next to her?

She'd fallen asleep alone. When she'd awoken, Giovanni was packing, so she scrambled to catch up and packed too, not wanting an excuse to be left behind. They hadn't spoken then, nor now.

She ruefully realized that she was climatizing to his silence, though it still wounded and unsettled her. Possibly his intent?

The relentless sun notched the intensity, so she squinted as the clashing colors blurred, assaulting her senses as they raced away from Nice. Her headache clamored into a migraine, the result of too much red wine the night before and no love. He drove relentlessly, elegant in Italian designer wear, deliberately unknown. The man she married was like an image in a luxury advert: handsome and unreachable. As she hunkered in the passenger seat, she worried that she was getting accustomed to being 'alone,' even when he was right beside her.

The car slowed. Joey watched through the Bentley's window as girls streaked down the Croisette on mopeds, their perfect, parted thighs clenching their machines. Giovanni stopped at the Carlton Hotel. The porters greeted them by name.

Upstairs, she walked naked across the room. Prowling like a tiger, he avoided. There was a time when the sight of her shoulder had made him hard. She turned in the window, the drink he'd given her despite the early hour, in her hand.

"How was she?" He turned away.

Had he not heard her, or had she not spoken?

She frowned, doubting herself. "How was she, Giovanni?" The delivery was no longer sotto, trying for conversational but unable to hide the edge.

He ignored her as though there wasn't a naked woman unraveling at his back - though it was his intent. The silence separated them. Deliberately. She understood that now and didn't know how to combat it. So, she crossed to him, pressed her naked body on him, and reached for him. He pulled her hand away, shredding her remaining dignity, igniting the long-held-at-bay anger. She stepped in front of him, grabbing his face hard, "Look at me. You used to love me."

"That was long ago," he'd spoken. At last. Confirmation of her fear.

She was not crazy. Her husband did not love her.

He turned away. She waited. Maybe he would speak again?

What to do?

She craved interaction and physical contact. Anything would be better than the isolating silence that disappeared her. Now, he had spoken she wanted the words to continue. Tentatively, she picked up her glass, hesitated, and decided. She rounded him - and tossed the red wine in his face, watching it cascade over his rigid features, soaking into his fine white shirt, waiting for a reaction. She hoped for anger that would lead to passion but noticed he was not aghast nor aroused. He moved unhurriedly.

Calculatedly?

He wiped the liquid from his brow. Granting her wish, after months of silence, he spoke spontaneously, and in so doing, he aroused her suspicion. A little smile flashed. "Let's not do this again."

Why the smile? And why was he talking again? Now? After the eternal silence?

She had hated his silence, but the talking was a sign. Something was about to change. She waited.

Would he speak again?

He continued dabbing calmly at the wine forming droplets on his sparse chest hair. He looked pleased but covertly so. She shook her head, not understanding the change or what was to come.

She returned to what she knew. This had been their thing. Live brightly. Fight formidably. Fuck ferociously. Repeat. Somewhere the fucking ferociously had fallen away. The bright living had taken on an exigency with no thrill, and make-ups, manufactured or real, never happened at all. Still, she would try. He seemed to be waiting for something. So, she tried what had worked in the past: Break up and makeup.

She hit him. It was not hard, but the sound was loud in the quiet room.

No reaction. No heated passion like their footprint from their tussles in the past. This had been their foreplay.

She scrambled back onto the bed, parting her legs, opening her nakedness to him. Thrusting her womanhood at him.

"Love me, Giovanni."

"No." He moved to the bathroom.

She scrambled after him, insisting, "I'm not crazy."

"Then don't act it." He shook her off, adding slyly, "Take your medication." He said it like planting a seed and watched her make the connections.

She recoiled, whispering the words this time. "I'm not crazy."

He raised his eyebrows. "Aren't you?"

She saw the provocation framed in his expression, quickly concealed. She backed away, trying to understand. What had she seen?

Triumph.

Her mind rejected the fleeting exposé but suddenly recognized, just out of focus, what he had planned in the months of psychological games that brought them to this moment.

This was an ending!

Her mind scurried for an act of normalcy so she could salvage her marriage. Her head was chaos, the migraine expanding.

She was not crazy. She'd read the signs correctly.

She felt fear.

Why had she provoked him? Maybe silence was preferred?

Docilely, she went to the balcony and stood bare in the bright traitor sunlight, seeing not the sparkling Mediterranean but looking into herself at the stretch of days where she'd been discounted, nullified, ignored, where she'd tried to respond to abnormal as normal.

When had normal frayed?

Sometime after she'd miscarried - but who wouldn't break at that? She'd plummeted into darkness and was given a little white pill to normalize. It had made her sleep and experience the world through a removed haze, a state she welcomed, especially when he'd layered the guilt for the miscarriage as hers and not an act of God. Being framed responsible when she was not, triggered her childhood, evoking memories she fought daily to ignore. So, for a while, she welcomed that little pill. But recently, she'd realized that her husband liked her sedated. When she tried to exert herself, he called her crazy. Joey began to wonder if she was crazy. She took on his truth. Had she been responsible for the miscarriage? Were all the things he told her about herself true? Was she wrong to be suspicious of the women who became part of their circle and then were replaced by a carbon copy?

Was it her?

She'd stopped taking her pill. She'd been determined not to be caught feeling. Reacting. Yet, here he was again, telling her their marriage failed - because of her. He seemed so certain. She felt confused.

What had she done wrong but mourn for an unborn child?

She was so accustomed to people telling her who she was and what she should do. She'd tried to please; she knew she had. She felt her youth close in. That old familiar feeling of disappearing in plain sight. Not heard. Framed. The injustice exploded in her head. She'd tried so hard not to feel, but now that she had, the emotions bubbled, clashing inside her head, mixing with the migraine. She became aware of an annoying guttural sound.

I did nothing wrong.

The sound made it hard to think.

It wasn't me. It was him. Everything I did was a reaction to him.

Her fury ignited. She clasped the stone railing as reality rushed at her. The guttural sound filled her head and blocked out her logic - unwittingly playing into his hands. The sound traveled with her as she barged into the suite. She picked up the poker next to the marble fireplace and attacked the locked bathroom door, calling him a coward, calling him out.

When he failed to do her bidding, she released her suppressed rage on his suitcase, then the mirror, the glass table, and the delicate French furniture, wishing someone would shut off the awful sound screaming in her head. She trampled through the splintered glass, trailing footsteps marked O negative in her wake until she stopped at the sight of a naked woman who looked familiar but for the wildness in her eyes and the blood on her feet. She began to shiver, telling her broken reflection the one truth as she knew it, "I'm not crazy."

2

THE HOUSE OF REST – 1985 ONE MONTH AFTER CANNES

The House of Rest sounded like some exotic club, but it was what the name intimated: a place to rest, talk, and be medicated. You saw the world through layers of gauze, and you never felt anything. Not pain, not joy, and you never ever wanted sex.

After months of compulsory confinement, Joey had felt calmer, but she strained at the restraint. White on white looked good in *Vogue*, but no human color made the mind do interesting things. It was like all the world's hues had blended together and solely lived in the eyes of the staff, as intense jewels floating in an achromatic world. The orbs looked at you but never met your gaze like you weren't really there. Joey needed to be acknowledged.

"Therapy is about trust," Dr. Brand had told her. "You can be open with me." It had occurred to her that she could say anything, and he would take it as truth. But she found that people believed you more if they desired you. She needed an ally. She needed to get out of The House of Rest.

Joey sat opposite him in her white skirt and waved her knees in and out provocatively.

"Why do you do that?" he asked.

"Habit," she lied. "I do it when I'm nervous. You make me nervous." She flashed her model smile. It was hard to remember to lie with the drugs crowding her mind. She'd hiked up her skirt, parted her knees, and adjusted her panties over her crotch. "Sorry.

I'm not supposed to do that, I know." She arranged her face into collaborative contrition.

He didn't react to her provocation. He looked at her for a long time. At her face, not the parted thighs. He was around forty. Hair trimmed but mussy over the crown. His moods were etched into his face - it seemed like he laughed a lot, frowned a lot, or maybe both. He was frowning now, touching the folder on his desk with his fingertip, delicate but definite.

"We have your file, Joey. Josaphina. I know your past."

She'd felt the cold shower wash over her.

Mother. Had mother intervened?

Joey stopped wiggling her legs. Joey closed her knees. Adjusted her skirt downwards towards them. Dr Brand saw her change from someone in control to someone on the brink.

"I know your obligatory time with us is almost done, but I don't think you're ready to leave, Josaphina."

And he was right, for all she desired at that moment was the sanctity of her little bleached room.

3

NEW YORK - 1986
SIX MONTHS AFTER CANNES

Joey was freed from The House of Rest. She was whole, with a little bottle of pills to keep her that way. She resented their power, the filtered life. She had spent a week at a Spa in the Hamptons and had arrived in Manhattan today, ready to live.

She climbed the stairs to The Agency. Claudia, the booker, embraced her while asking after Giovanni, though the answer had been splashed across all the tabloids: **SUPERMODEL TRASHES ROOM, DIVORCE TO FOLLOW. MILLIONAIRE MOVES ON. MODEL DRIVEN MAD BY DRUGS.** The last was particularly ironic because she had been driven mad due to a lack of drugs – lithium in particular. In this world, it is better to be addicted than have a sickness. Everyone knew that models survived on cigarettes and blow. There was no shame.

Claudia eyed her professionally. "You still look great. You want to work?" Joey nodded, aware that age was now a factor. She was 27. Claudia leaned in, cupping Joey's cheek in her palm and whispered, "How long will it take?"

Joey knew what the booker was referring to but feigned ignorance. "How long?"

"The weight. Before you lose it? What are you? An eight? 125?"

The six-footer looked at the plump booker, squat like a half-crushed tomato. No one was telling her to lose weight. "I'm a six."

"It has to go." Claudia smiled, her eyes hard, her voice adamant.

their collision didn't knock her down. He grabbed her with both hands and looked into her eyes.

She did exist.

The twisted mouth asked, "You okay?" The voice was deep, like good cigars, whiskey, and wood crumbling in a grate, lubricated with just a hint of foreign.

She lied and said, "Yes. I'm fine."

He looked at her closely, and a light turned on in his eyes, turning them from onyx to rich chocolate. He recognized her. The cruel lips morphed, showing uneven white teeth, making his smile more interesting.

"Can I buy you a drink?"

"No."

He was embarrassed. It was morning. "I'm sorry. Of course not."

He frowned. She looked into his eyes as the wind whipped platinum fronds across her face, obscuring her wretched condition, repackaging it as appeal. Joey wondered if, along with the recognition of who she was, came the recollection of what she had done: The headlines and tabloids of her screaming adventures in Cannes? She searched his expression, waiting. Joey and the stranger, the only stillness on First Avenue, wrapped in a gust of wind. He looked north, unsure, then dug in his pocket. His hand emerged with a card. His eyes asked the question. Her hand answered, taking the card. His cruel lips, now kind and curved.

She walked to a phone booth and took out her book of contacts. She needed contact. Joey slipped in her quarter and dialed.

"Hello? Darcy? It's me, Joey. Remember?"

There was silence, and then the anger rushed through the line like a hurricane. "Fuck you, Joey. Remember? Who could forget?" The line went dead. Joey hung up. Pleasure on her lips.

Who could forget? She had. She had forgotten. Darcy! She dug at the memories of light and shadow, unclear, indistinct flickering negatives on a jumpy projection of time, of lips and bodies, of hookups and breakups.

Darcy had been the one who had introduced her to Giovanni. How could she have forgotten? A sound broke from her lips; it was as sharp as a burp, unpleasant, yet perversely pleasing. She remembered the thrill of the chase, the triumph of success. A threesome turning into a twosome. Darcy had never stood a chance. Joey had made Giovanni her own.

Until he no longer was.

He'd moved on to the next carbon copy of Joey. The tabloids were full of photos of Giovanni and a starlet named Jane canoodling on a yacht. Jane looked exactly like the blonde seated next to Giovanni that night at the dinner before the Cannes debacle. Joey made sure to avoid the blaring headlines of her life. Her mood shifted from triumph to pain. She clutched her phone book and pulled at the Louise Vuitton as though she could escape her mind by moving.

Joey had not been crazy. Extreme manipulations evoked extreme responses. No one had asked why she had acted as she had or if her behavior was appropriate given her treatment by the man who said he would love and cherish her always.

If Giovanni had been upfront when it was clear that the marriage was over, she would never have found herself in The House of Rest. Instead, he had played her in a way that unraveled her for reduced alimony. He had made her invisible. Included her, but never addressed her. Started conversations with others while she was mid-sentence in one of her own. Walked from the room when she'd tried to address him.

Every action amplified what she knew to be true but which he refused to discuss. That the meteor blazing a trail across the heavens - and tabloids - catching everyone's stare, that had been their relationship, had burned out faster than either had thought it would.

His mistake had been to marry her. Hers had been thinking that when the glitter no longer hung in the sky, they'd be kind to each other. Live an arrangement. Retain a relationship. They'd never discussed the end of their marriage before it began. They'd both been high on life and coke, he in impeccable velvet Gucci, she in a sheer lace mini by Vaulton - before he was famous. The hangers-on crowding into the Las Vegas chapel to witness an impulse with consequences no one wanted to consider. The last months had been a chess game with him waiting for the queen to fall. Unwittingly, she'd played his game without understanding the strategy. Not a queen, but a pawn, easily taken.

The endgame? Six months in The House of Rest - Giovanni's leverage in the dissolution of their marriage. A diminished Joey equaled a decreased alimony.

As Joey cut across 57th, headed west, she found herself facing a row of tabloid covers stretching across a newsstand. She halted her combat with Manhattan's populace and stood looking at photo variations of her former husband and Jane embracing on a yacht, with herself as an insert in a circle in the corner of the frame.

The sight revved her disconnect. Her insides felt like they were on the outside, flying through the air, hitting the high-rises and the passersby. She felt herself disintegrate at what had been done to her, and the proof of it splashed in public, like strangers' fingers invading a raw wound. It made her crave the sanctity of The House of Rest and the soothing tones of Dr Brand. It took her to that feeling that overcame her on the balcony in Cannes, which had resulted in her internment at The House of Rest.

***

Joey could not move, mesmerized by the proof of her husband's exploitive play, exposed. Yet no one seemed to register what the headlines proved. She wanted to yell her truth to the world, make them hear her. Believe her.

I am not crazy! It happened. It was him.

Tempered by the truth.

No one would believe her.

She felt the desire to crumble where she stood. It felt like the world had tilted, and she was about to slip into an altered reality. Joey needed to feel safe. She needed someone who would shelter her.

She walked away from the jeering headlines with apparent purpose, but no destination. The scat-jazz of New York City making it hard to think. She needed a friend. Who might take her in? Gia was dead. Joey had to be careful not to imitate her friend.

Who would shelter her now?

Joey hadn't been home in a long time and was in no condition to break that pattern in her current need. She'd inherited her looks from her father and her ability to stay afloat in a wash of Champagne or Vodka from her mother. Joey was trying really hard to resist that cure. Going home would tip her back into a bottle.

The mere thought of her mother's eternal dialogue framing Joey's failures was enough to nix that idea. Mother had relished the collapse of Joey's marriage as proof of Joey's inability to sustain. Joey needed a shitload of narcotics before undertaking the maternal embrace of those cadaver arms, and right now, she was clean, even of lithium.

The noise of the cars darting like sperm up the Avenue, cutting each other off in pursuit of space, pounded at her. She couldn't think. She needed white, the repast that The House of Rest had fed her. Joey hailed a cab.

***

The Essex House Hotel was respectable. A good place for quiet. The rooms were so goddamned dark, though. Nothing white. She looked in the mini bar, caressed the little bottles of alcohol with the fevered touch of a lover returning, lingering, then quickly slammed the door shut, leaving them as cool carcasses in their darkness.

Joey moved to the phone. She needed a friend, not a parasite. Her book was filled with people who had moved on and those who never cared beyond the allure of her status, which had crumbled thanks to Giovanni. She loved like she lived. Fiercely, consumingly, destructively. So, her field of friendship was arid, with her, the forgotten scarecrow, the buzzards hovering in the half-light, with no one to shoo them away.

She flipped her book closed. On the back was a name she couldn't forget and a number she'd half-remembered. Her lips puffed, and her tongue darted between her teeth. Pride at having kept Fran's number flashed as a feral expression.

Fran. Solid citizen du jour. Fran. Blonde in the way of a farm girl. Freckled. Fuckable. There was no way she had moved. Fran had secured an apartment before going to the parts of America where no one ever went to look after her dying mother. Joey had lingered in New York, suppressing cognizance that she did so in anticipation of Fran's return. Then Giovanni had happened. Years had passed. By now, Fran's mother had died. Surely? So suckable Fran had to be here in Manhattan. Almost touchable. Joey ravished her lower lip and traced the numbers with her fingertip. Fran. She picked up the phone and dialed.

4

FRAN

Fran was in the kitchen preparing dinner when the phone rang. She answered it, poking at an asparagus spear, cradling the phone in the crook of her shoulder. "This is Fran," she said in her chirpy, no-nonsense voice. A thousand memories douched her in the husky voice that filled the room, but really, just her everything.

"Fran? It's Joey, remember?"

Fran stepped away from the hot water softening the skin of the vegetables and looked out the kitchen window. She stared across the metal sky penetrated by fortresses of cubicles people called home. She looked beyond the East River, across the Atlantic, to Europe, to the Pension Haben, and to Joey.

"Joey." The word felt foreign on her tongue.

"You remember?"

"I do. I remember," she spoke cautiously. "How are you?" The banal is always a good safety net.

"You don't read the papers?" Joey's laugh, all hot embers.

"I do."

"Then you know."

"Yeah. I guess."

Fran sat down in the window, examining her feet. Naked in the heat of the furnace. Vulnerable. She stretched out a leg and hooked on her Chinese slippers, "How did you find me?"

"I kept your number."

A vacuum, as Fran thought what that line meant. Joey paused just long enough to let the compliment of that statement penetrate, then added, "Yours was the only one I kept."

Fran straightened on those words and moved out of the kitchen until the stretch of the telephone cord stopped her. She stood there at the end of the line, not looking at anything, remembering Joey.

"You still modeling?"

"Aren't we all? But yeah. I also graduated. A degree in design. Clothing. I always wanted to."

"I remember you had a way of putting mismatches together like an exotic bird, making people want to touch you."

"What do you mean?" Fran was not going to play.

"To feel the fabric. You always wore 'fuck-me' fabric. Do you still?"

"Joey."

"Well, do you? I think you'd make a great designer. I'd let you undress me. I mean, you know. Dress me."

Fran turned and walked back to the kitchen briskly, collecting the telephone cord like a lasso. "Damn."

"What?" The humor coating Joey's words.

"My vegetables burned."

Joey laughed, an open, joyous sound that she hadn't made in a long time. Fran stopped jabbing at the asparagus with the spatula and paused to listen to the magical music of Joey's laugh. A soft smile of tenderness overcame her. The feelings of Hamburg showered her.

Joey's voice was intimate. "I meant what I said. You'd be a great designer."

"We'll see. Modeling is good for contacts. I learn wherever I can."

"Funny. I never found great contact modeling," said Joey, deliberately misunderstanding. "It's what I lack. It's what I crave. It's why I search. It's why I called."

The silence stretched again. Maybe this wasn't a good idea. Fran moved, monitoring the moods coming into the air.

"I'm kidding," ameliorated Joey. "You still with the same agency?"

"Yeah."

"Nothing, if not predictable." The words shot out sharp, and Fran could hear the regret when Joey spoke again, fast. "Sorry. I don't know why I said that." Fran could feel Joey's restlessness. "Maybe I wish.... Whatever."

Another long silence. Fran waited. She was going to proceed carefully. Everyone who knew Joey knew what she was. Joey evoked visceral reactions in Fran; disruptive, like metal clanging on metal in blackness, the sparks spectacular, but the source, leaving welts. Fran had deliberately chosen to disassociate from Joey's effect. She had stamped their primal connection with a vanilla label acceptable to society: Fran liked Joey. There was something of the broken bird about Joey, which awoke the protector in Fran. But she wasn't naive. She was nice. There's a difference. Joey was a disruptor. The silence elongated as their history in Hamburg pulsed.

"You seeing anyone?"

"Mike Malone, the photographer. We're engaged," Fran spoke hesitantly, expecting to be berated, slipping a naked foot from its heat and exposing it.

Back in The Essex House, Joey frowned. Her first 'go-see' in New York, almost a thousand years ago, ended with Joey and Mike in the sack. His elemental energy made women want to rub against him like a cat against your calves. He was easy sex - no expectations. He was not the kind of guy Joey could see married to Fran. Joey wondered if Mike would remember her.

On the other side of the line, Fran was relieved by Joey's lack of response. It gave her the strength to say, "I've got to go, Joey. It was good talking to you."

"I'm in The Essex House. Call me."

"Bye, Joey."

"Promise." Insisted Joey, knowing that if Fran promised, she'd have to call.

"I promise," said Fran. She pressed the button on the phone, ending the call.

5

CHOICES

Joey flexed her toes at the thought of meeting Fran and Mike again. She wondered if Mike had changed. Had he become loyal, or would he hit on her like he always had? If he did, that would get complicated. She pushed the recognition aside. Life was picking up. She went over to the mini bar and grabbed two J&Bs. She cracked one, her mind skipping, wondering if her old dealer was at the same place and confident that the problematic eight pounds would be but a nightmare thought, come next Tuesday.

She lay down on her bed, raising her legs like two sticks of dynamite ready to blow. Then she spread her toes with their red nails framed against the black ceiling, like ruby-jeweled combs stabbed in a geisha's hair, and she knew she would be fine. She reached for the little white bottle of lithium on the side table and swiped it into the trash.

Joey walked down Park Avenue along the painted lines between on-coming traffic; the horns were a symphony of acknowledgment that she existed. She didn't care for the lithium cobwebs that had cluttered her mind. Somewhere between First Avenue and the non-conversation with Fran, she decided that if she had to survive on drugs, they would be her choice of drug, not from a prescription from some doctor that doused feeling. She'd become a cover girl, superstar, on coke. It was life without drugs that made her cartwheel into craziness. Her choice was clear: Live life through Lithium layers of padding and disappear in the crowd, or assert herself.

But could she assert herself without the little white pill?

She jiggled like a dancer between the careless cars. The headlights spotlit Joey like a showgirl in Vegas. She stretched her arms to the ink-splattered sky with sugar granule diamonds twinkling in its depth. She stopped, arched, and smiled as the traffic played dodge-'ems.

"Crazy broad."

"Stupid bitch."

She closed her eyes and opened her ears, letting the traffic's song obliterate their words. Then the traffic stopped, and she crossed the road to the sidewalk and felt alive.

When she was four, before her father died, he raised her on his palm, straight above his head. Joey, a little blonde bonbon, quivering with pleasure and pride at his strength. She teetered there, on his hand, alone in the air, breathless from the fear of falling but somehow safe in his hand, knowing that nothing would ever go wrong as long as he was around. When he died, she tried to recapture that thrill, but she was too big to fit on anyone's palm and never trusting enough to feel even partially safe.

6

JOEY, FRAN & MIKE

Joey pressed her lips together over a tissue, leaving them moist as though kissed but not ravaged. She pulled into second-skin jeans and tugged on snake-skin boots, which were well-worn and more beautiful with age. Brown, cream, black – the little triangles that gleamed so slickly on the snake, now curled away from the core as though repulsed by what they encircled.

She pulled a snug T over her nakedness, emblazoned with the message: *I'm not crazy, you're not sane*, written in high-rise letters across her breasts. She bent from the waist, combed her hair from the nape to the floor, then tossed it back full and fluffed. Carefully, she softened the pencil line around her eyes with a brush. She wanted to look careless – which took a lot of care.

She was nervous. She hadn't seen Michael or Fran for how long? There were reasons. She took the little bag of blow and walked the length of the new apartment she'd secured the day after Fran had called. Usually, finding a place in Manhattan took time – or money. She had money. Her stay at the House of Rest had ensured that the payday of marriage to Giovanni left her with more padding than her Connecticut heritage had, but not as much as she would've had had she not succumbed to his manipulations. She could afford to buy what she wanted. The apartment was bare but for a bed. The Louis Vuitton open on the floor. Her clothes dropped where she'd removed them. Furniture wasn't a priority. The wooden floor and the light from floor-to-ceiling windows enough for now.

She loped in long, loose strides, her boots thunking on the wooden floor. She led with her pelvis, her legs bent at the knee, the gait unnatural and awkward. A vulnerable smile came to her eyes. She hummed softly, remembering Hamburg, as she moved through the elongated reflections from the giant windows onto the hardwood floor.

1976 - HAMBURG:

She and Fran had created that walk with the South African in the fall leaves of Hamburg, singing some stupid song. The words escaped her, but the tune remained. The air that day was frigid, threatening snow. The South African had never seen snow until she arrived in Hamburg and was stoked at the prospect of it snowing again. She was excited like a kid in Candy Land. Fran had taken the South African under her wing, as she was want to do with any stray thing in need. Joey had resented it.

The three girls kicked the fire-hued leaves crumbling beneath their feet, their arms hooked into each other for balance, their legs overlapping diagonally. Step left, step right, faster and faster, singing that ridiculous song. Fran's hip rubbed front and back, front and back; her thigh on top, her thigh beneath. Her freckled face flushed in the ghost's-breath air. The South African pretended to sing the words, laughing until she dropped. Fran pulled down next to her, then Joey, deliberately, atop them both, laughing on a street in Hamburg in a tumble of arms, legs, and soft breasts.

"Get off!" They pushed her, but she refused to go. Spread eagled on her back, Joey floated on top of them in the icy air while the leaves rose and fell. Girl smells, girl giggles. Soft. They flipped her to the side, and she rolled onto her belly. They crawled on their elbows, looking at her, mouths open in pleasure. Not fake like in a shoot – real. Their joy was like a thing, a blade that could slice you. Joey felt the cut as they got to their feet, unaware of what their bond did to her.

So she did whatever she did when she felt. She destroyed the moment. She tackled them, ramming at them like a linebacker. She launched at them with arms spread, but they danced out of her trajectory, and she landed on her belly in the leaves. As though pre-arranged, they hooked legs on her legs and held her down. Inner thigh on back thigh, hip bone into buttock, grinding unconsciously in their play to keep her pinned. They covered her with bonfire leaves. Joey lay with her head in the dark foliage, her legs spread and held down, the soft hands roughly drowning her, and she felt now again as she felt it then, a raw thing – joy. It was pure. Like getting a ride on Daddy's back, him a horse on all fours, she astride, feeling the muscles beneath her hands – the rhythmic gate as he crawled, and she yelled, "Gee-up! Daddy." Happy and aware that she was safe.

***

JOEY'S APARTMENT:

The memories got too close. She straightened, the little bag of blow held in her pointer and thumb. She raised the bag up high to the right of her vision. She saw it peripherally, then closed her eyes and let it fall as she pivoted. Plop. It landed in her left palm, and without looking at it, she curled her fingers closed, like a Venus Fly Trap, engulfing its prey. The cocaine tucked away from sight, clasped tightly in her fist if she should need it. Joey opened her eyes. It was time.

***

FRAN'S APARTMENT:

When Joey knocked at the apartment door with its wreath of berries yelling 'domesticity,' she avoided the direct view of the peephole. She leaned her head forward so her hair curtained her face, keeping her eye on the little glass circle in the door. She wasn't going to be seen without seeing. The peephole darkened. Joey scratched her crotch.

The locks clicked as Joey quickly struck a pose, spreading her arms on either side of the doorjamb, throwing a cocky grin on her face as the door swung open. The air went out of Joey, overpowered by the image of long ago, of naked limbs alabaster in the candlelight, of gentle movement becoming frantic, followed by soft sighs of release. Suffocated by the visual, Joey didn't know how she stayed erect.

Fran used the door as a semi-shield. Her face was partially covered, her hair knotted and twirled in an alluded to bandana of vibrant colors splashed against silk, playing peek-a-boo through the blonde tumbles. Her white shirt was exquisite, tailored to fit but not restrictive. Open to the curve of the breast, brown and full. The skirt was what? Wool? A cashmere blend? It looked rough and smooth simultaneously. You wanted to dry hump it. Fran's feet, hidden in Chinese slippers.

Joey and Fran regarded each other assessingly before their apprehension morphed into delight. Simultaneously they embraced, clasping greedily. Joey frowned, gripping tightly, wanting to consume Fran. Wanting to hurt her for her contentment. Forgetting that while in the throes of her Italian passion, she had never called. She had only thought of Fran in the most abstract way, like when she came from masturbating or made a list of people to hate.

The orchestra of locks performed a brief sonata behind her, and they were through the twilight hall into the magic of a blood sky, peppered with planes and high-rises and the black cold of the East River. Even Joey lost herself in the sight, seeing nothing but the mobile heavens. She felt alive and wanted to live in the moment forever. Fran to her left, magnificence everywhere else.

"Beautiful, isn't it? We arranged it for you." Mike's clipped Canadian tones lacked timber, the forced words covering his awkwardness, layering lightness as a disguise.

Michael was seated with the light behind him, so she couldn't see his face. Was that planned? He struck a match; the Irish eyes he got from his great-grandmother glowed enigmatically in the flame. It was a telling look in its ambiguity that took a moment, read a volume, and had no doubt, given his tendency for theatrics, been planned from her call to accept their invitation. The look was one of collusion. *He had not told Fran that they had fucked.* In that brief flame-illuminated synapse, a world of unguarded, unsaid words were communicated in disguise. There was evaluation on both sides. How had they changed, and something else, intimates, like in a conspiracy. Then, the memory that they were not alone.

Joey's eyes flew to Fran, who was watching Joey, her expression blank. Joey wondered what she had revealed in that unguarded look with Mike. She glanced back at him, but the flame had gone out. He was once more a silhouette with a circle of light from his cigarette.

Fran felt a sliver of ice slide down her back. She was right there, yet she was on the outside. She was the link between them, yet somehow felt excluded. In her own home, she should feel comfortable, but what? It was a feeling of undercurrents.

Joey turned to her, and for the briefest of moments, Fran thought she saw something; then Joey's mask came down, and the moment was gone. Joey clicked her heels, military style. Gesticulating at the view. "Awesome, guys!" Then she turned with a false enthusiasm, beckoning at Fran. "Come, do the walk, do the walk!"

Fran looked at her vacantly, still trying to figure out what she'd just seen. "Walk?"

"The Hamburg walk! The silly-song walk!"

She said it like Fran should know exactly what she was talking about.

Joey bent her knees and took an exaggerated right step, an exaggerated left step, and hummed off-key. It came back to Fran. Hamburg – autumn leaves. Joey removed and cagey until the South African fell.

Joey grabbed Fran around the shoulders and did the bent knee walk, forcing Fran along. Fran couldn't help herself. She hesitated for one moment, then she was doing the awkward step, singing, 'Love Potion #9.' They strutted across the silk carpet, then broke apart, wriggling and gyrating. The revelation that had almost happened already forgotten, just as Joey had hoped.

Mike watched in the shadows. Joey! Of all the people to manifest. Joey. Images of their former intimacies flashed in his head: Joey arched over him, blonde hair drowning him, breasts smothering him, holding him down, riding him. Fast, hard, rough, not like a girl. Her eyes closed like she was fucking someone else. Humming.

"Look at me," he pleaded.

Her mouth open, face contorted, pounding on him, her breasts bouncing in his face.

"Look at me!" He grabbed her face, and she opened her eyes and looked at him.

She slapped his face hard, then her hand palmed his throat and pushed down so he struggled to breathe, his eyes widening.

"I can't breathe." He gasped, but she smiled and pushed down harder, still arching, riding faster, that weird monotone humming. Joey's yelp of joy across the room echoed Mike back to reality.

He stared as the two women slithered against each other, singing the stupid song; Mike wondered if Joey had had Fran, too? There was something in the way they touched. Sensual, innocent, but specific. He felt his hard-on press against his jeans. Fran and Joey going at it. That was something he'd like to witness. He adjusted his erection. Maybe he could participate? Mike, Fran, and Joey. He felt his mouth go dry at the thought.

The women broke apart, laughing and gyrating. Like foreplay. Then they stopped, faces close, mouths open, breathing hard. Separate but close. Michael waited. He must've groaned because each turned to him, Joey's eyes were filled with laughter, Fran's expression concealed - not a look he was accustomed to from Fran.

She stepped away from Joey, reverting to the straight Frannie he knew.

The concealed look now open and benign. Fran moved so the wing-tipped chair was a barrier, shielding her from both Joey and Mike. He shook his head. Nah, he must've imagined the moment, colored by the memory of Joey. Fran would never agree to a threesome; she was too straight. He'd made the suggestion before, and she'd said no.

Joey grinned, moved to Fran, and draped a straight arm over Fran's shoulder. "What's a girl got to do to get a drink around here?" She challenged. "Mike, you gonna satisfy me, or you just gonna sit there and watch?"

Fran's eyes flew to Joey. Had she heard right? Again, she looked at Mike but couldn't see his expression. It was her turn to wonder what had leaked out in the uncensored moment. She donned her Chinese slippers as though they were her shields. Something disruptive was happening, and she wasn't going to let it. "Mike, ask Joey what she wants to drink; I'll get the hors d'oeuvres from the kitchen."

Joey met Mike at the 50's Sinclair antique bar cart. As he made Fran's drink, he whispered, "What are you doing, Joey?"

"Did you tell her?"

Having her next to him was bringing back too many memories. His blue eyes met hers and dropped to her mouth and then to her breasts, nipples piercing the words: I'm not crazy. You're not sane.

"No. Did you?"

"No." She watched his gaze linger on her breasts, and her eyes narrowed. She did a slow serpentine roll with her torso so her breasts raised, spread, and settled back in place. He couldn't help it. He literally licked his lips. She grabbed him by the arm, sounding angry, and hissed.

"You gone honest, Michael?"

He moved his chin at her. "Why are you asking?"

"Just yes or no, Michael. Pick one."

He didn't know what she was asking, what he should say. What was the right reply?

He opened his mouth to answer as Fran flicked a switch illuminating the living room, placing a charcuterie on the table. Mike closed his mouth. Pivoted. "Want a cocktail or wine?" Mike moved away from Joey towards Fran. The air felt charged, like before a storm, and he wondered what his reply would have been if Fran had not interrupted them.

7

JOEY - THE SEDUCTION
TWO MONTHS LATER

Men.

Joey was shooting with Mike in Fran and his apartment. She had not lost the extra pounds, so working despite not hitting the emaciated target dictated by her booker, was a power move. Usually, a booker would not put you on the books for work until you reached the target weight, but if a client called and asked for you specifically, then The Agency would not refuse work – and a commission.

Since that moment in the apartment with Fran, with Mike's gaze like a touch, Joey had been watching Fran's fiancé. More accurately, she'd watched him watching her, with Fran right there beside him. It made Joey wonder what Mike was doing when Fran was not there.

Usually, Joey wore jeans and a tee for a shoot. Today, she chose spike heels with ties that wrapped around the ankle and elongated up the mid-calf. Her sage skirt had a little slit that revealed the entire length of her never-ending thighs. She added a V-necked cashmere cardigan that clung to the curve of her breasts – the top button left undone. She was like a living example of a graphic novel's illustration of what women looked like. A nerd's fantasy come true.

Joey brushed her lids with a pale plumb that read natural. This was a small job. Catalogue. No hair or make-up provided, so she'd done her own. It would be just Mike and her. Alone.

The shoot went easily. Four looks. She could have done it in her sleep. Mike up close, behind the camera giving instructions. "Sexy. Yes. Open your mouth."

"Does Sears do sexy?" asked Joey, knowing that the catalogue house served middle America and wholesome was the image.

"I want to use some of these shots to pitch you for another client." He answered reasonably.

"Wait, let me straighten your blouse." He leaned in and stroked a breast, his excuse to smooth away a not-there wrinkle. "Better." He breathed. Their eyes met, and he dropped his and retreated behind the camera.

When the shoot was over and she was changing, she looked up and caught him watching her in the mirror. It wasn't accidental.

Something clicked in her brain. An idea. She curved her back so her short skirt tilted up towards her butt, legs straight and parted. She leaned forward and picked up her cashmere top from the bed, slipped her arms in the sleeves, her breasts bulging, and squeezed between her upper arms as her forearms and elbows were restricted against her waist in the soft, narrow fabric. She stopped and looked up. He was still watching her. Neither moved.

She'd been right about Mike!

She waited until his eyes met hers in the mirror on the wall so he knew she saw him watching her. Then she raised her arms over her head and jiggled so the sweater slid down over her naked torso. When she emerged from the sweater and looked in the mirror, he was gone.

She busied herself packing away her model bag of accessories. The thought that had entered her brain when she caught him watching her expanded. Fran was her friend. Mike, it was clear, was still Mike. She already had proof of that, but the gratuitous adjustment of the blouse made it clear that little had changed about Mike when he took Fran as his fiancée. Her brain clanged the alert she'd been suppressing. *Mike didn't deserve Fran.* Joey made a decision. Time to test truth – or was it testing lies?

She entered the living room with long strides, heel first so her legs didn't bend at the knee, model bag slung over her shoulder.

"Coffee?"

"I should get going."

"Stay." She faced him. He looked away. Squirming. "Have coffee. Stay."

I regret nothing. I don't believe in regret. You can let that cancer suck you up, so you're not living, just regretting. My theme song is 'Non, Je ne Regrette Rien.' On bad days like today, I will play the song in full decibels and perform a pagan dance to the trilling of Edith Piaf.

She dropped her model bag where she stood. "You sure?"

"Yes." The reply came fast, without any consideration. He hadn't moved.

I will not regret that I didn't scream the first time he touched me in the dark, making my mother acknowledge that her little girl was engulfing things no little girl should struggle with alone. Wanting to please, knowing it wrong, being assured it was right. Dealing with the hardness in the softest of places that hurt from the size that gagged the child in the release.

She strolled lazily across the gleaming floor to bask in the watery sunlight. She stretched like the figurehead on the prow of a ship as thunder clouds raced across the New York sky.

"Don't," his voice croaked.

"What?" Joey's face was innocent as she turned and looked at Michael's frustrated expression. "Don't what?"

I will not regret that I did not report the man who trapped me in the dark supply room during my summer job, where he defiled me repeatedly; my code of silence so ingrained that I never spoke of it.

"What you're doing," said Fran's fiancé. He had not moved from his position after the offer of coffee, like his feet had grown roots, and he lacked free motion.

Joey balanced against the windowsill, considering his words, figuring his play, her legs spread for balance, her short skirt riding her thighs, the little slit revealing more. She leaned her back on the ice glass, her nipples pushing through the thin, white wool.

"So, no coffee?"

I do not regret leaving my mother without a word, drowning in her sorrow, aging in a bottle, poisoning her life with guilt. I turn my head, profile, so my back arches a little as I look out over Manhattan, the buildings like erect penises prodding the swirling sky.

"You're like – you're like Elizabeth Taylor in 'A Cat on a Hot Tin Roof,'" he spat, as though the analogy was an insult.

She brushed an imaginary fleck from inside her thigh, her hand unconsciously stroking the muscle. She frowned. "Elizabeth Taylor? She's short and dark; I'm tall and blonde? Where's the comparison?" When he failed to respond. "Anyway, how old are you? Who knows that movie?" Her eyes were not kind.

I don't regret using my body to get the things I thought I wanted. I don't regret that once I had them, I tossed them aside like broken shells. I don't regret that I seldom feel, for when I feel it is with blades unsheathed that cut the entrails of my life, so I lie whimpering, aborted in the wake.

"You're like a cat. That's what I meant. And I'm the tender vittles you're trying to taste. Always brushing up against me, touching me, like you do it unaware, but I know – I *know* it's calculated."

I assess him. This nothing man. This excuse for a 'y' chromosome. Weak. I lean forward and the V of my knit moves away from my body as my breasts swing forward with gravity. I give him an excuse to be a real man. Though I know he will not take it.

"Never once since I'm back, Michael. Never once touched you, nor tried to. Never. No enticement ever."

I look directly at him, over a shoulder. No expression. Just leaning on my knees. But. You know. Men.

He reached to the heavens, calling for understanding. Making his excuse for what he's always intended to do. "There! Right there!

You're doing it again." His voice close to breaking. If this was captured, he'd get an Oscar.

To the casual eye he appeared frustrated, exasperated. But what was the impetus? He'd forgotten that she knew him and was immune to his act. She knew his ploy and had rejected his prompts since her return. Mike's frustration was that he was not driving the outcome. This was supposed to be easy. She was making him spell it out.

I feel the power as I linger on my parted knees, holding onto my smile, holding onto his gaze. He still had choices. He could be an honorable man. He could look away.

Joey picked up the conversation, though he'd forgotten the last line. "Doing what, Michael?" she asked reasonably. "I'm not doing anything. I'm merely sitting."

"It's *how* you are sitting."

"How?" Joey laughs. "Are you weak, Michael?"

"No."

"Then what's the problem?"

"There isn't one." He sounded confused. Defeated.

I do not regret what I am about to do. What I feared I might have to do since I heard the news that this reject of humanity managed to convince the finest person I know that he would be loyal, that he would be a good citizen, that he would be a stalwart husband. When I knew he would not.

Joey straightened. "You never made the debate team, did you?"

He wanted to retort but nothing came to him. He felt like a cornered animal, immobilized, unsure to pounce or retreat. Joey had always been the aggressor, and she wasn't playing to form. It was her move. That's how it had always been with them. Yet Joey remained across the room.

"Did you say, I wasn't sitting right?" she asked wide eyed, the epitome of reasonable innocence. When he didn't reply she shrugged. "I mean, how *should* I sit?" She challenged him. "Want me to wear a burka, Micheal? Want me covered? Cloaked?"

He could leave. He could turn away. There were a million things he could do. He did none of them. He stood where he was, saying things he didn't believe, looking for an excuse to do the thing he'd wanted to do since that moment at dusk in the living room, when Joey had walked through the apartment door.

She pushed off the windowsill. "Want to tie me up, Michael? Restrain me?"

I regret Fran. Of all the things in the world that I could regret, I regret her. Not the experience of Fran. God, no! For that was heaven. That was pure. Fran could have saved me. Life with Fran was a Jacques-Louis David. Life without her was a Pollock. And that was where I floundered now. My chance with Fran was gone and I had grown accustomed to my life. My path provided no detours. I was on an extended cul-de-sac. But I would not stand by and watch the one good thing in my life that had not erupted like red paint splattered across a white wall, be destroyed. Not by him; a man unworthy of Fran's love.

"Everything you say.... It's like a game."

"What's the prize, Michael? Me?" She shrugged. "You've got your woman. Don't play. I'm not asking you to. I'm telling you: don't."

I'm giving him every chance to make another choice. I know all the words are an excuse he can placate himself with later. The bulge in his pants a beacon saying I'm right. For all his words, my instincts are right. I remind myself of my intent and how I came by this intent on a street in Manhattan.

So, do this now, for it will happen later when Fran has kids, and a ring, and a life woven in infidelity. It will happen that crushed promises are believed, traded for the honesty of admitting that this man is incapable of monogamy. This choice was not Fran's smartest – it was her weakest. She will accept the pretense when he tells her that he'll never break her heart again, rather than fragment the family and admit she was wrong to believe that he could change. He will contaminate her with his lies, so she becomes the opposite of fine. The non-Fran. So hurt her now. Educate her now. Wake her now.

I look down the tunnel of time to see where this road will lead. I have walked the path of pretense. It took me to The House of Rest. I see their future written and produced, starring Fran the Pure, and Michael the Foul. So I regret nothing as my heels click on the hardwood floor. I stop before Michael, not touching. Just waiting for the touch I know will come. He is not who he pretends to be. He is disposable.

Am I?

Action versus inaction. I gather up my fears and put on my cellophane armor. I'll be fine. I'll do what I've always done: destruct and derail; no one expects more. I'll bring him down. And should she turn to me in her time of pain, I will take a chance and feel. Expose the wound I keep hidden. Try love again, knowing that in so doing, I invite the quicksand of the baying hounds that seduce me evermore toward my terror of returning to The House of Rest.

Joey stopped a foot in front him, and repeated. "Don't do it, Mike." Her white teeth sank into her full lower lip and she grinned.

***

MICHAEL:

She's in front of him. Finally. Not touching him. He could walk away. Should walk away. But the memory of her. The actuality of her. Who would blame him? He moves. Grabs her at the nape, claims her mouth, his other hand slips between her thighs.

8

BETRAYAL

So they made unspectacular love. It wasn't even like the thrill of newness could add excitement – she'd had him before, often. This was a mercy fuck. When the act was over – and it was an act for her – he was anxious for her to be gone.

"Fran could be home anytime."

"Funny how you only recall that now." Joey pulled on her skirt. "I'll make the bed – you shower."

You could see his mind working the angles. Was she too obvious? He was sure to check if she left any tell-tale signs. Damn! She hated to think the whole exercise was done in vain, and since she'd volunteered, she actually had to make the bed. It wasn't something she ever did, but like most things in Joey's life, if she wanted to, she could do it perfectly. She glanced at her watch, "I should get going." She bent down and picked up her top from the floor. Suddenly, he was Mr. Charm.

"That was fun. Maybe we could do it again?" He snuggled up behind her. "And this never happened, right?"

"Right."

"It would hurt you as much as me."

"You think?"

His eyes tried to penetrate her expression.

"Go shower," she remarked playfully, bending over straight-legged like a stripper. She peered at him from over her shoulder as she straightened the bed linen.

Being a man, he immediately forgot his thoughts and grinned at the view.

"Go shower," she said again, and he disappeared.

Quickly, she pulled the duvet over the rumpled sheet, fluffed the pillows, and stood back to admire her work. She did a good job for someone who never made her own bed. A great job! She removed her earring. Should she leave it beneath the pillow for Fran to find? She tapped the beaded jewelry in her palm. She'd purchased the earrings years ago while she and Giovanni were sailing the Med in their first throes of passion. When she'd thought she'd actually loved him. She gave a mirthless laugh. No, she couldn't get away with anything too obvious, not after the look on Mike's face when she offered to make the bed. She yanked a long blonde hair free at the root and left it on Fran's pillow, which she indented slightly. That should do it. She became aware of the silence ringing from the bathroom. The shower had stopped. She better get out of here. Just one more thing to do.

***

Michael pulled on his jeans, questioning himself. Why had he done that? It was almost the only time he'd been unfaithful since he and Fran became engaged. Sure, he'd done the newbies while they were dating, but since he put that ring on her finger, he was only unfaithful once, and that was an accident anyway. A fresh face who looked at him like he was God. Today was all Joey. He always had a thing for her. She knew just how to get him going. He liked that she was always in control. He should never have taken the chance and hired her for the campaign. Fran insisted, though – never sensing the threat. That was what he loved about Fran. She saw the good in everyone. Even Joey. Okay, even him. It never occurred to her that the Joey she saw was not the Joey everyone else saw.

"Don't judge her on what others say." Fran had counseled him. "Judge her on who she is."

He almost put cologne on out of habit, but that was a sure sign that something was awry – a shower and cologne in the middle of the day. But with Fran, he could even explain that away if he had to – he'd say that he'd exercised – he didn't usually, but it wasn't out of the range of possibilities. Fran had no reason not to believe him. Anyway, it wasn't really his fault. He'd had no choice. Joey had made him. She could be a classic bitch if she was bored. He wouldn't be surprised if she'd slept with him just to fuck it up between him and Fran. So why had he done it? Because he could. She had crawled under his skin and arched and sprawled so he was thinking with his dick instead of his brain. He knew it was dangerous – but he enjoyed the illicitness of it. It added spice, and Joey was always fun - she knew just how to get him off. No one would know. But he was no fool. Joey never volunteered for any sort of labor in her life. She was up to something. He exited the bathroom.

"Hello?"

No answer. His voice reverberated in a way that suggested he was alone. He did a quick check, padding silently on bare feet. The apartment was empty. He looped back to the bedroom and stared at the bed. He had to be smart. He chuckled. Conniving bitch – he went over and smoothed the pillow free of the subtle dent. Slid his hand below, swishing the sheet for hidden objects – none – but the sheets were rumpled. He flipped the duvet back. The scrunched sheets would have given Fran something to think about. She made the bed herself that morning. She was a neat freak - organized - always hanging up and packing things away. Joey knew it and had deliberately tried to arouse her suspicion. Well, she'd failed. Screw you, Joey, he thought in triumph, then noted - he already had.

***

Joey hummed in the back of the cab. She felt good. She had just done her friend one gigantic favor. The booking she'd just had with Mike would also send a message that Joey was back, desired, wanted, and available for hire. The Agency would have to overlook the 3 pounds she was unable to shed. She survived on a water, lime and vinegar fast, whittling away five of those last pounds. The final three remained stubborn. Still, they were all in her boobs and a little in her butt. The clients wouldn't care. By being hired before her target weight, the booker couldn't insist on those final pounds disappearing before putting her name back on the roster. She'd a *fait accompli*. Two birds with one stone, so to speak – and she was still off blow.

9

A DAY FULL OF SUNSHINE

When Fran got home, Michael was all over her. They made love right there, balancing on the back of the loveseat. He took a while to come, but that simply elongated her pleasure. They moved from the living room to the bedroom. He ripped off the covers, pushing her backwards onto the bed; spreading her and eating her. When he finally came, they showered clean together and made the bed. She felt him watching her closely until she placed her hands on her hips and asked, "What?"

"What, what?"

"Why are you looking at me like that?"

He wore a sexy grin. "Just realizing how lucky I am." He walked over to where she was standing, and she turned to enter his embrace.

"Only realizing that now?"

He kissed her. "Can't a guy give his girl a compliment without getting the third degree?"

"Sorry."

Fran knew she could be a little stern. Men had complained that she tried to act like their mother instead of their lover. Picking up after them, trying to get them to eat better, be tidier – she'd better watch herself.

"Do I mother you too much?" She couldn't keep the hint of concern from creeping into her voice.

He knew he had her. "Mother me? Hon, if my mother was anything like you, I'd advocate incest."

"Michael!"

"C'mon now, mommy. What are you making me for dinner?" He kissed her neck. Her fears rushed away.

"How does baked salmon in a white wine sauce sound?"

"Hmm, delicious – and if I don't finish my din-dins, will you promise to punish me like this?" He swatted her gently on her behind.

"Hey, buster, watch it!" She grabbed his wrist, wriggling away from him, laughing as Michael gave chase.

***

Fran was working for the designer, J.P. They'd met in Hamburg through Charlie, before the couturière's name had become an international brand. He'd hired all the models from the Pension Haben for his German shows. Charlie had met him in Paris, and through her help, the girls from Pension Haben became part of his early crew. When J.P.'s clothing became the choice of stars on red carpets and was featured in all the top fashion magazines, he'd still used the girls from Hamburg in his campaigns. J.P. was no insecure prick. He knew Fran had aspirations of becoming a designer. He knew she had dreams of dressing the working woman who couldn't afford couture. He allowed her to watch and learn, a gift no designer ever gave away. He also still used her in his fashion spreads from time to time.

When Fran got home from the shoot for J.P., her freckles had been covered, and her hair stood like a bush of wheat around her head. Her eyes kohled, and her mouth shimmered in liquid gloss. She wore a tight white mini that showed her skinny frame and iron nail hips. The cream-knit leggings clung to her lean thighs and disappeared into her three-quarter calf boots.

Efficiently, she went about the apartment, picking up the clutter Mike deemed unnecessary to discard. His beer bottles from the night before, the yellow boxes that his film came in. The coffee mug balanced upon her collection of classic magazines. She grimaced at the coffee stain circled on a black and white vintage cover of Twiggy. He could not get it through his head that these were of value to her. Irritably, she tossed the magazine and decided to leave his mess exactly as it was. Fran entered the bedroom. The comforter was lopsided, and the pillows askew, but right in the center of the dishevelment was a note.

Fran. Every day with you is a day full of sunshine.

She smiled. That was the reason she was with him. No matter what anyone said, and everyone had something to say, they didn't see this side of him. All her rancor receded. She smoothed the sheets, straightened the bed covers, and accidentally bumped into the side table, scattering the 'Thought For the Day' cards that she flipped through each night before sleeping. They were self-fulfilling prophecies and reinforcements. *'Life is good.' 'Enjoy the moment.' 'Seek not what you do not have; seek instead the joy of what is tangible.'* So he was messy, but he was Michael, and he was hers.

She dropped to her knees and scooped up the cards, forming a neat pile. She bent down on all fours and looked beneath the bed. She lowered her head to the carpet and stretched her hand, scooping up the cards; she glanced at the one on top.

Life can be a hike or a stroll – it's how you view the journey.

She smiled. That was true. She put it at the bottom of the pile of cards. Looked at the next card:

Do not ask for everything, yet do nothing to obtain your desire.

That's why she was hanging with J.P. He was willing to help. He was teaching her. She made a note to sign up for some additional business courses at The New School. Before placing the inspirational cards on the bedside table, she gave one more cursory glance beneath the bed. She was about to straighten when something shiny caught her eye.

10

CONSEQUENCES

"Maybe it's not what it seems." Joey knew it was exactly what it seemed.

Fran grasped at the lie, desperate for it to be true, then discarded any excuse with logic. "I've gone through every scenario. No way an earring can get beneath the bed unless someone was in the room," she frowned.

"Could a model have changed there?"

"Sure, if she was stripping for him. We've agreed no shoots will ever take place at our apartment. It's just not possible."

"Maybe he brought home accessories for a shoot, and that's one of them.

"Do you think that sounds believable?"

"Question is, do you?"

"What can I think?"

"My experience is anyone can think anything if they want to badly enough. What do you want to believe?"

"Truth isn't like that."

"Yes, it is. 'Cause this truth isn't about him, it's about you. How much do you love him?"

"I love him."

"Enough to lie to yourself?"

"No."

"Sometimes truth hurts. It rips away pretense, and you've got to be strong enough to take it. Or strong enough to pretend to believe the lies. So I ask, how much do you love him? Enough to give him another chance and accept whatever explanation he gives you?"

"I'd never lie to myself."

"No?" The question came with the heavy weight of knowledge. With all the understanding of the shadows, the ones she and Fran had once played in. Their secrets, always hidden by a fabrication of truth. Joey reached out and stroked Fran's hair, "You ever tell yourself the truth about us?"

Fran got up and walked to the black and white pictures in silver frames clustered on the mantle.

Joey stood behind her. She lifted the weight of Fran's hair in her hands and smoothed the wheat strands down her back.

"Fran, you, of all people, can live a lie. I know it; you know it. The question here is, will you live this lie? And if so, for how long will you live this lie? And. At what cost?"

"Joey?"

"Yeah?"

Fran had picked up a photo from the mantle and was staring at it, not listening to Joey. "This is you in Europe, right?" Fran's voice was tight, flat.

"Yeah."

"On the boat?"

"Yeah. The yacht."

"Before the – before The House of Rest."

Joey smiled. "You mean before I was misdiagnosed? Sure, why?"

"Nice earrings."

Joey felt her heart explode in her chest. "What do you mean?"

Fran held up the earring she found beneath her bed. "What I said. Nice earring. Thought it looked familiar."

Joey felt the same terror that struck her in Hamburg the day Fran had left on the shoot after tossing the Turk from Joey's bed. It was a knowledge that something had irrefutably changed. "What do you know?" She tried to keep her voice steady. "This looks like the one I used to have. I lost them – god knows how long ago."

Fran's freckles dominated her face. "You wore them at the coffee shop this week."

"Did I? Nah, I'm sure I lost them a while back."

Fran poked a straight finger at Joey. "Prove it."

"What do you mean? I can't turn back time."

"Nothing so sci-fi, honey. Show me your jewels."

Joey looked directly into Fran's eyes. "Why?"

"To see if there's one missing."

"I keep lots of earrings, even after I've lost one."

"Bullshit. Joey, you do this, or we're done. Got it?"

"I can't. I left my accessory box at my last shoot. I still need to go get it."

"Liar!"

"It's true, I've not had time to get it."

"Liar." Fran turned and headed to Joey's bedroom. Joey tried to intercede, but Fran was quicker. Fran scouted the room and eyed the multicolored beaded box. She had picked it up in Morocco a decade earlier as a gift for Joey. Their eyes landed on it simultaneously. Joey ran to it as Fran reached it.

Joey placed her elegant hand on the lid, a hand that had been featured in some of the top jewelry ads for the most exclusive jewelers. Remember the campaign with blue hands clutching green breasts – full and round – the fingers splayed against the round softness; the fingers layered with enamel rings and diamond bands, bracelets like cuffs crawling up her wrists? That was Joey. Joey's hands. Joey's breasts. The campaign featured body parts and jewel-encrusted hands holding, probing, and stopping the onlooker in their tracks. Now, they attempted to stop Fran. Fran was not dissuaded.

"Fran?" Joey pleaded.

"Open it." Joey clutched the Moroccan creation the way Luke Sky Walker grasped his saber.

Fran's chin came forward, as did her hand. Quite simply, she smacked the box from Joey's clutches. The jewels spiraled upward and outward, the throw-away baubles along with the inherited pearls.

They fell with little thuds on the dresser, onto the unmade bed, sliding across the slithery sheets, skidding across the wooden floor. Fran scanned the expensive debris. She lurched onto her hands and knees and came up with the matching earring in her hand. She placed them next to each other on her palm. "You don't need to fuck everyone who loves me."

Fran stood. Joey hadn't moved.

"I love you too, Fran."

"Then the trend is complete. You just fucked yourself."

"This wasn't for me. It was for you."

"Isn't it always?" Fran tossed the delicate beaded drops on the floor and headed for the door.

Followed by Joey's voice, "We're still friends, right? I mean, we'll work this out?"

"No, we won't. We're done."

***

FRAN:

Fran stood for a long time on the corner of Central Park and 57th Street. She walked fast through the crowded street, mind blank, unable to string concrete conclusions or suggestions. *Walk*, she told herself. And she did until she didn't anymore.

It was only when a gust of wind pushed an empty Doritos bag across her vision, snapping in her face, that her thoughts returned. Fran moved, a humorless grin crevassing her freckled face. A man coming toward her thought it might be a smile and slowed with a questioning curl to his lips. He fastened on her eyes and felt his stomach constrict, for the expression was feral. He recoiled. Fran continued, oblivious to other's perceptions. Not beaten. Not broken. Moving.

Neat and tidy as always, Fran folded Mike's clothes, piling each fine garment upon the next: From his Calvin Klein jeans and Ralph

Lauren denim shirt to his Armani cashmere coat and sweaters. She put as much as she could into two suitcases and dragged them to the elevator.

The view from the roof was spectacular. The wind wiped the sky clean. She took a moment to admire the beauty. She then opened the suitcases and placed piles of Mike's clothing on the roof's boundary wall that established the perimeter of the high rise. She divided the clothes into four neat piles on each compass point and then returned to her apartment with the empty suitcases, and waited.

Fran stood in the window, munching on carrots. She had experience with crisis. She avoided confrontation whenever she could. Confrontation brought back her childhood. The shot. The blood. The wounded man with his face half missing that had once been her father. Mother and Frannie, shocked and relieved. *Accident.* Know your line of defense. Deny, deny, deny.

A gust of wind pushed up against the building, and two of Mike's shirts sailed by like spent condoms, empty, discarded, and so appropriate.

The sound of the key in the door made her turn her head expectantly. The doorknob rattled. The bell rang. Fran picked up another carrot. The phone rang. She bit into the carrot. On the fourth ring, she answered the phone.

"You *are* there." Mike's voice rushed at her through the telephone.

"Yes."

"The door won't open for some reason. Let me in."

"I changed the locks."

"What? You – why?"

"Your clothes are on the roof."

"Roof?"

"You don't need to repeat everything I say."

"You're not making sense. Open the door. Talk to me."

"I am making sense, so listen before I hang up. Your clothes are on the roof. If you want them, you better get them down before they blow away." Stunned silence. "I know."

"What? What do you know?"

"You and Joey."

He didn't reply on point. "You can't change the locks. I live here, too. Let me in. I want to see you."

"Name's not on the lease, buster."

"Frannie, let me in."

"Don't call me Frannie."

She hung up the phone.

He knew better than that. She hated the name Frannie; it's what her father called her.

Forty-five minutes later, there was the sound of metal on metal. Fran looked through the peephole. Mike and some guy working on the lock. Fran opened the door. "What the fuck do you think you're doing?"

"Thanks, pal." Mike handed the locksmith the cash and walked past Fran. She noticed a pile of clothes beneath his arm and a bundle on the hallway floor. He did not take the time to pick them up and give Fran the chance to shut the door again.

He walked to the center of the living room, dumped the clothes in a chair, and turned, legs parted, hands on his hips. His blue shirt opened a button too far, the beads around his neck glistening at the throat. His cuffs pulled back; his thighs flexed. He displayed everything she was throwing away, and she still had not met his eyes. His long hair fell in loose curls to his shoulders, and his eyes, the color of a bright spring day, beamed rapprochement. "Can we talk?"

"No. I found the earring." She saw his mind search for meaning and then return innocently to hers with a shake of his head.

"And that affects me, how?"

"Joey's earring."

He knew that it was important to maintain a neutral expression. He tried to still any outward movement. Innocent. He told his body. Innocent!

"Good. Was she pleased?"

"Under our bed."

He furrowed his brow. "Okay. And?"

"And? There's only one way it could've gotten there."

Yeah, and he knew exactly how. The bitch *had* been playing him. He took a silent breath and willed every molecule of his body to a state of calm. His voice tried for frustrated patience. "I'm sure you're gonna tell me what this has to do with you placing my clothes on the roof and changing the locks 'cause I'm seeing no connections."

"You slept with her. Fucked her. It's the only way the earring could've gotten under our bed."

"Whoa!" He held up reasonable hands, palms outwards like she had a gun. "That's some extrapolation." He stepped toward her and chuckled again, relaxing his body visibly. He reached for her, and she slapped his hand away. "Frannie, that's just not true. There must be some other way for her earring to get beneath our bed."

"No."

"Yes. Think about it. If I was going to sleep with – it even sounds stupid to say – one of your friends, would I do it where we live? In our bed? Where you could walk in on us at any time?"

Fran's brain darted along the path he was leading, trying to hit the suggestions out of the ballpark. He seemed so reasonable. Unfazed. Did a guilty person act this way? *You did*. Noted her inner voice. She ignored it.

"Didn't you take her on a tour of our place that first day she came over? Didn't you guys sit on our bed and look at old pictures together?"

Fran flashed on Joey stretched over the bed, head propped on her hand like she was doing a layout for a photo shoot. When the bed had gotten too full of memories, they had landed on the floor, backs against the bed, talking until Mike had joined them.

He watched Fran replay the memory and knew that by her considering it, he had already won. It was in the erectness of her body, like a tulip too long in a vase, the stem slumping, the bloom disintegrating; that was Fran as the piss and vinegar dissipated, and his words made her see what he wanted her to see rather than what was there.

"That must've been when Joey lost her earring," he stated triumphantly. Michael could see he was winning. "Why would finding her earring make you think - ." He paused to show his distaste, then shook his head in disappointment at Fran. "Fucking Joey? Of all people?"

He baked the sentence in a humorous syrup of disbelief, like you use on a precocious child when they say they don't believe in Santa, and you ask, "Then who eats the cookies?"

"Because I've cleaned a million times since then and never found the earring."

"You hear yourself? You overlooked an earring, and that somehow leads to me fucking someone I've had so many ways? Someone I have no interest in ever doing again?"

Fran looked at him. He knew he'd won. "The only reason I took her photo was 'cause you begged me to 'Help her.'" He waggled his head, imitating Fran. "Now suddenly I'm the schmuck doing your friend in our bed?" He made a sound like a snorting horse. "Y'know, maybe we're done."

"No."

He'd half turned away. Now he stopped, his smile hidden, before turning back to her. "And what's with the clothing thing? Hope nothing's lost, that's all I can say."

"I'm sorry."

"You should be. What did Joey say?"

"She denied it."

He felt relieved. "You owe her an apology."

Fran's mouth tightened.

He picked up the phone and held it out to her. "Call Joey. Now," he spoke sternly.

***

Fran stood with her head bowed, knowing she was emulating her mother.

"Do you want me to dial, or will you call Joey yourself and apologize for the ludicrous accusation?"

She looked at Mike but didn't see him. She was in a hidden corner of her brain, in a place she hated to go.

11

FRAN - KENTUCKY

Fran sat next to her mother, listening to the death rattle. Her mother's dancer legs retained their shape, though the skin bagged around the knees. Her hair was streaked gray like parts of her had died, leaving silver strands of decay to show you can't cheat Father Time. Fran smoothed the damp cloth over her beloved mother's face. If she had known, she would've returned home sooner. The girls from Hamburg offered to come with her, support her, when she'd discovered what her mother had been keeping from her. However, this was private, and she wanted to do it alone. She should've returned when her father died and seen for herself how her mother was doing, but she couldn't. Fran – who could handle anything, could not stand at his graveside and pretend to grieve. She couldn't bring herself to say 'goodbye.' Not to him.

Fran's eyes settled on the frame on her mother's nightstand. Her father, white-blonde, handsome, tanned in the way of a construction worker. Her mother in her ballet stance within her father's embrace. Each parent resting a hand on Fran's shoulder. Fran's freckled face smiling, but her eyes were watchful. She reached for the frozen moment as her mind flew back to her childhood.

The bell – a figurine breaking – sounded, and father was out of his corner, fists raised. The bout had been brewing for weeks, and he was more than ready to fight. He was the favorite, and he moved confidently, shoulders hunched, neck tucked. He'd beaten this opponent before and relished the skirmish. Boys spend their lives banging against other little boys in sports, settling fights, and then they reach an age where they say, “Stop, you can no longer let your frustrations out this way.” What’s a boy to do? Where’s a man to go when the world has its foot on your neck? Where to find a worthy opponent – one who will not sue?

Dad danced forward unsteadily as though punch-drunk; fists bunched. He had been in pain for a while, tried everything to alleviate the animal inside. Tonight he knew he would get satisfaction. In the big fights, like Mohamed Ali’s World Championship bout, the ring is aflame with lights, with noise thundering beneath the blaring announcer. The crowd spurring the ref to keep things fair. This fight was silent now, as though society had gasped at what went before and was afraid of what was to come. Where was the ref keeping things fair? Nothing below the belt, no blind sides, never hit a woman. That night, it was just me, hoping he’d lose.

The words flung back and forth as the whiskey disappeared. At one point, I tried to whisk the bottle away, but he saw me and stopped me. Mum distracted him so she remained the target. The room magnified: to my right, father oozing malignancy, to my left, mother, resigned. The smashed figurine – the one of the ballet dancer, delicate, graceful, that mum got when she passed her ballet exam at age ten – symbolized so much about the marriage. The differences they thought they could overcome, visible in the room at odds with itself. Dad’s hunting paraphernalia marring a wall as decoration. Mum’s Degas reproductions on the opposite wall; a house divided. Hers, his, I left no imprint. Her delicate furniture, his lazy-boy, her *Time* and *Newsweek*, his *Hunting Today*. Her first ballet shoes – bronzed, his first Armadillo – stuffed.

When the action began, it would arc or collapse. When it was over, he would be free of self-hate for a while and he went back to being my dad. Did mum love him? Could she still, after all the put-downs and smackdowns? The lies of continued love, as though Fran was not there, hearing the noise, sometimes seeing the sights. Which was worse? To witness or hide in my room? In the dark, with the senses straining, everything is bigger. You try not to hear but you hear it all. She wanted him to stop.

There's a part of us all that does unimaginable things in our dreams. His darkest dreams became truth. Me, I'm daddy's girl. I'd been having dreams, too. I'd been dreaming of this dream for a while. Most of us keep our dark dreams in a box 'cause if you let them out – well, there's some things that can't be undone. Mum's nose will always be skew. Her figurine will always be broken, and love can become a lie.

My dream I let out of the box.

People hide bullets in the back of closets because if bullets are not in the rifle, no kid will choose one and load it. Dad gave me two skills; the one came as advice. One morning, after another prize fight with mum's beautiful face, distorted and colored in a way that thunder clouds look before a storm, her movements slowed with pain, my father gave me advice that has stood the test of time. "Frannie," his voice a deep rumble, "deny, deny, deny."

"What does that mean?" He looked down at his open knuckles, pulling his mouth down to the side, "It means I never meant to. It's not deliberate. And I'm sorry for what I didn't know I was doing."

"Deny, deny, deny?"

"Now you got it. If you do something wrong and never admit it, it never happened. Like when you broke your mother's favorite figurine."

"But I didn't," I interrupted.

"That's my girl. Deny, deny, deny."

Dad also taught me to shoot.

Afterwards, the two gifts together saved me. "I'm sorry, I didn't mean to. I didn't know it was loaded. I wanted him to stop, but I would never hurt my daddy. He never hurt me."

"Deny, deny, deny." I did. They believed me. Life went on.

***

NEW YORK CITY: FRAN'S APARTMENT

Fran straightened but didn't look at Michael. "I'll do it myself." She moved to the phone and dialed Joey's number.

12

FEEL

Joey lied all the time about little, unimportant things, like the time she told the South African back in Hamburg about her 'sisters' when she had none. Well, none that she knew of, but how would her lie change the South African's life? It hadn't. Not really. Charlie wanted to go down a path. She took Joey's lie to make the journey easier. For Joey? Lying was the lubrication of life. Even if you didn't lie, everyone thought you did, so you might as well. Joey lied by omission, for control, because she could, and also because it was fun. But she never confused truth and lies. The lies she told hurt no one. They added color to life.

Fran was a whole other story. Part of Joey knew that she lived the lie of Giovanni because Fran could not face the truth of Hamburg. The House of Rest, the lithium, the subsequent fracas? It had been a fog to cover the lie that Fran perpetrated. Joey had tried to get Fran to talk about the truth of Hamburg, but Joey didn't have a good track record with being heard or believed.

She'd tell the truth and be accused of lying. She'd tell a lie, and everyone believed it as the truth. Back in Hamburg, she'd slept with Charlie so Fran could see the South African as she really was: molded by the current. Nothing special. Charlie's purity was about lack of exposure, not choice. Joey slept with Mike for the same reason - to prove a truth - and even if it killed what the two women secretly had, Joey thought she'd done the right thing if it meant that Fran saw Michael for who he was. By doing what Joey had done Fran could not hide from the truth about Mike.

Then the fucking phone call.

"Joey, I'm sorry. I should've believed you. Forgive me."

Sure. Why the hell not? What was the point to keep at it? As she had listened to Fran's voice through the phone she wondered what had gone down that she was getting this false apology. People believed what they wanted to believe, regardless of proof. Proof and lies. Story of Joey's life.

Joey got up and did what she always did when she needed to think. She walked down the length of Central Park, past Hotel Row and the horse-drawn cabbies. Then east, to the brownstone that is 'The Agency.'

She hated returning to 'The Agency,' past the calculating eyes of the Next Big Thing. They checked you up and down, looking for flaws. Their eyes screamed: *Move Over. You've had your time in the sun. Old woman, get out. Make room for me.*

Claudia, the booker, air-kissed Joey.

"Darling, the clients are lining up. ESTRA is looking for a new face for its mature line. I've submitted you."

Bitch! Bitch! Bitch!

"Thanks, sweetie. If I get any samples, I'll pass them your way. The crow's feet are still there even when you stop smiling."

She knew she shouldn't piss off her booker, but the bitch was submitting her for the face of the MATURE line. Joey wasn't yet 28. She would talk to Paulo, the head of 'The Agency'. She needed someone who was really on her side. Someone who would be more nurturing. Claudia was still harboring a grudge. Apparently, the 20% she got from Joey's earnings was not enough for her to pretend to be nice.

"What's coming up?" asked Joey.

Claudia flipped open her booking calendar. Most days had huge crosses on them with designer names people paid thousands to wear, indicating work she'd been booked for, along with magazines like *Vogue*, *Elle*, and *Allure*. The booker perused the pages. "Pretty solid for the next three, four weeks. Why?" Then, fear popped into the booker's eyes. All she needed was for Joey to flake again.

"Just asking." Joey smiled sweetly. Let the bitch worry a little. Actually, the knowledge that Claudia had already booked her for the upcoming weeks gave Joey the power to threaten to leave – that way; she could renegotiate the percentage she paid the agency. She smiled sweetly. *Gotcha! Be nice to me, or you'll be gone, bitch.*

Maybe the booker read something in her eyes because she asked Joey unexpectedly, "A bunch of us are going to a private fundraiser for Alzheimer's tonight. It's at that Producer, Sammy Waltz's place. Want to join us?"

This was a higher-tiered 'meet and greet' situation where photographers, clients, models, and playboys got together at some super exclusive event. Young, hot, hip, the connected, and the rich. One alone was not enough. You had to fall into several categories to be included. It was always fun to see who turned up and who left with whom.

"Sure. Why not?" She shrugged. Never appear too eager.

"A car's picking up Roger du Donai around 9:20. Okay if you share it?"

Roger du Donai was a star athlete. Gorgeous, sexy. No, she definitely wouldn't mind sharing a ride with him. "Make sure I'm picked up last," warned Joey. There was no way she would be kept waiting in some limo until someone else deigned to join her. If anyone was going to be late, it would be Joey.

***

Joey paced the wooden floor of her living room instead of getting ready for Sammy Waltz's party. Once back in her apartment, her brain kept Fran's apology on rotation, pure disbelief fogged logic and dampened feeling. She felt that old familiar disconnect. "What the fuck?"

Fran's apology meant that Fran was going to stay with Mike. Joey had gambled and lost. She hadn't anticipated that the earring could be traced back to her. Fran's apology played in Joey's head for the millionth time as she looked unseeingly into the unceasing activity of Manhattan. She examined the 'phone call from Fran again. It came out flat, like a bad recitation at a school Eisteddfod.

"Joey, I'm sorry. I should've believed you. Forgive me."

Joey ran out of floor to pace, and whirled back towards the center of the room. She felt like those pictures of soldiers who return from war with their arms and legs missing - amputated or blown away. That's how she felt. Unhinged. Like feeling had been liquidated, cut out of her completely. It was worse than the Rivera. Even if the pain of her miscarriage and Giovanni's subsequent behavior had provoked her breakdown back then, it was still *feeling*. Now? Joey was numb.

How could Fran be so stupid as to take him back? After all the effort Joey'd put into showing Fran who he was, what he would ultimately do to her? The words kept repeating in her mind, *"Joey, I'm sorry. I should've believed you. Forgive me. Joey, I'm sorry. I should've believed you. Forgive me. Joey. I'm. SORRY!"*

Joey collapsed her torso into a 'C,' feet planted, thighs flexed, fists balled. She yelled a guttural sound of frustration and disbelief at New York City, but the city ignored her. She was accustomed to the response. She straightened, hung her head, and conceded: Fran had chosen Michael over Joey. Joey had hoped Fran would turn to her for comfort. That she and Fran could live their happily ever after. Instead, Fran had chosen to believe a lie.

***

The leather mini barely covered what needed to be covered. Joey pulled on a soft suede halter fitted so loosely that when she leaned forward, you could see her breasts, as though by accident but not accidentally. Joey gnawed her fat bottom lip. What was astounding was that her fuck ups were so carefully thought through. However, when the outcomes got corrupted, she didn't lie to herself. She owned her mistakes. Back in high school Joey had decided that if she participated in the choice, she was still in control - wasn't she? She couldn't look at that assertion now and label it true. She never seemed to have control of outcomes. But she was discovering, since Europe, that she was capable of deliberate choices. Not good ones, but choices she thought would achieve her goals when she undertook them. She always believed that her good intent would manifest in her desired outcome. She never considered what would happen if her objective failed. The House of Rest prompted her to ask herself questions she'd never thought to ask.

The buzzer interrupted her self-discoveries. The static voice announced the arrival of her car. "Be right down," Joey chirped, deliberately obscuring that she was so far down on the emotional scale that she couldn't sink much further. Joey didn't move.

Feel, feel, feel.

The mantra replaced Fran's apology in her brain but failed to impact her disposition, so Joey changed the word and replaced it with the instruction: *Connect.*

Mr. New York, Roger du Donai, needed a fresh face, and she needed a distraction. Men always thought that they were the ones pulling you in. Man: the moron. It never occurred to them that women might have an itch that they're too lazy to scratch. Sometimes it was less effort to bag a boy with a reputation for being something big on a screen or stage, than going to the trouble of sweating, so you came alone. Sometimes alone is where it's at. Tonight, in her disconnected state, she needed people.

The buzzer burped again. She didn't move. She hadn't been this close to taking a hit since walking the traffic of Park Avenue that first night back in Manhattan. She'd had the blow all this time; she just hadn't needed it. Tonight, the need was overwhelming. In her silver heels, she tapped across to where she left the white powder before first visiting Fran. It seemed like a century or more ago, but in reality, it was just a few months. She knew she shouldn't take the hit. She whirled away, doing the stupid Hamburg walk, singing "Love Potion # 9." When Joey stopped, she was at the bureau on the far side of the room again. She retrieved the little bag that she'd tucked away in the African ebony box with its hidden draw. She trailed a line and then one more.

The little gold straw - standard - everyone had one. She held one perfect finger against her nostril and inhaled through the other. Pow. But she didn't feel. One more. She shook her head and caught her reflection in the cold black glass - a screen to the life of the city, the place where energy pulsed in promises of mobile veins of traffic and helicopters and people on the streets. She refocused on her image in the glass, ensuring no white rims hinted at her hit. She sniffed deeply, ran her tongue around her gums, fluffed her hair, and glided into the night.

***

He was a big dumb jock with tight curls and muscles, who grabbed her thigh and said, "Yeah, baby." He gave her the furrowed brow smirk that made a million girls cum, but left her cold. Still, a jock was a jock, and a notch was a notch.

There was nothing to talk about, so he pulled her over, and they chewed face for a while, and just like that, they had sex. She straddled him on the back seat until he came. She guessed that the driver had watched in the review mirror 'cause the partition wasn't closed, though the driver averted his eyes when she slid off Dumbo, cleared his throat and asked discretely, "Would you like me to drive around again?"

They looked out the window and realized they were 'here' wherever 'here' was.

"Nah," said the jock without checking with her first.

She dabbed at her crotch with tissues she found next to the cut glass decanter before they stepped from the car into the flash of light bulbs.

"Roger, over here. Joey, you back?" The press scrambled for the shot.

This was the reason they were here. Du Donai was making a foray into endorsements, and being paired with Joey made people think of him as more than just a jock. Joey needed the jock to prove she was back, that she was desirable, and that she still had 'it.' They were interchangeable to each other.

They posed for the cameras as though just for the hell of it, but with a purpose. Her leg hiked up with his jock-mitt on her thigh, two beautiful people that the rest of the world wanted to be, but were not willing to pay the price in the flesh and heartache it took to be them.

Joey needed something. She felt compressed, like she was in a cube where people moved and shouted, and she'd gone deaf and couldn't feel. They went up in an elevator. She didn't ask where they were going. Instead, she rubbed up against him, and they kissed. They entered a penthouse with lots of candles and strangers who knew them both.

"Baby," she syruped, "good to see you. Again."

She kissed the air next to a trillion faces and whispered in the jock's ear, "Who are these bozos?" and "Score me some coke."

He introduced her to some guy with a receding hairline and a big nose and a bigger belly. He had short stubby fingers that dug into her flesh as he said, "I see you in all the magazines. You want to act?"

"I do every day in bed." Deadpanned Joey.

He laughed. "Maybe I can audition you?"

"Not likely."

"Just kidding," said the man with his shirt open a little too low, a lot of hair showing between his plunging collar.

"You look like a bear," Joey noted. "Do you hibernate?"

"You on something?"

“Yeah, and I need some more.” He nodded, his pudgy hand on her backside as he guided her through the crowd, his free hand parting the crowd like Moses and the Dead Sea.

“Feel free,” she stated to no one in particular, then laughed at her own joke. ‘Free feel,’ is what she had meant to say.

He guided her into what looked like a British library, all old wood and books. It reminded her of her home in Connecticut. He moved to the bar, his back to her. He picked up the crystal decanter filled with amber liquid; his body so massive it obliterated his actions. The sound of ice dropped into a glass telegraphed the unseen ritual.

I know how ice feels. The thought flashed in her mind, replaced by an image of Fran. She didn’t want to go there. She didn’t want to be in the room with this gross guy. How did she get here?

The man took his time, like pouring a drink was some sorcerer’s art. Finally, he turned with a beverage in each hand, rotating the liquid so it swirled in the glass with diamond patterns etched into it. For a moment, the liquid looked cloudy, but when he placed it in her palm, it was clear, and she thought it must’ve been an illusion of the subtle light.

“To you.” He held his glass aloft. When she failed to toast him back, he closed the distance between them, lifted her hand with the glass in it to her mouth, and said, “Drink.”

The blow had had no effect. Maybe whatever was in the glass would?

The glass emptied, she moved to the books. “You ever read any of these?” Her hand snaked up to the beautiful spines, touching them, trying to connect. Again, the memory of the library in the home of her youth. The recall provided no comfort.

“You read?” He said, like a challenge.

“No, I’m a model, remember? I don’t have a brain.” He doesn’t laugh. His mind was focused on his goal. She became aware of him behind her, his hand moving inside her halter. She stepped away.

“Blow,” she said the word with the same command that he used when he’d uttered the word “Drink.”

He misunderstood and assigned his desire to her. He pulled at his fly so she could blow him.

"Not you. Coke," she corrected him. "I'm supposed to be the dumb one here." She turned and walked back to the party.

The jock was snorting from a table in front of what looked like a real Renoir. There were old hags and beautiful young things and famous faces. A well-known movie star from two decades ago lowered her head, revealing a wrinkled, sun-damaged décolletage, as she leaned forward to take her fix.

Joey was about to reach for the jock when she saw his eyes focus, and she followed his gaze. Across the room entered a petite black woman, Kohled eyes above a heart-shaped, lip-glossed mouth. Her hair a huge halo of ringlets, like an unsexy Donna Summer. She wasn't beautiful, but she was famous in the way of being on the short list for the upcoming Oscars, famous. That would be history-making if she was nominated. The previous year, Whoopi Goldberg had been only the fifth black actress to get a nom for an Oscar since its inception in 1929. Joey didn't know why she knew that fact, but she knows her status as a model no longer counts. In the world of the beautiful and the known, you are only 'it' for as long as the moment before someone hotter, more famous, more connected entered, then your cachet tarnished, and the new bar was set. The hunters got out their dicks and the game was on for the new quarry and the bet was out for the least time it would take for one of the power brokers to bag her.

Joey's head suddenly felt like it had exploded, and globs of debris were fogging function. She grabbed a glass of water and walked to the garden rooftop. Sheila E.'s 'The Glamorous Life' blasted across the black and white marble. The beat felt like it throbbed in Joey's brain. The patio, deserted. The air, cold. Joey wondered if Fran was fucking her photographer. She realized she felt discombobulated, out of it. Not just numb, but woozy. Maybe the combo of blow and whatever Stan gave her in the study? She walked to the corner of the terrace, trying to clear her head and looked at the clouds covering the stars, and then she looked down.

Vertigo assailed. She was so high above - in height not blow - and beneath her, a miniature world. Movement everywhere.

Jump.

She recognized the urge. She needed The House of Rest and the whiteness bleeding all color from the world. She turned away from the beckoning void and saw a phone next to one of the semi-damp chaise-lounge cushions in front of a tree with miniature oranges, so small, Joey at first mistook them for objects d' art.

Call Fran.

The thought percolated and wouldn't leave.

Call Fran. Call Fran. Call Fran.

A waiter with actor-like good looks offered her a shot from a silver tray, but the world swirled, and she knew she was in trouble. She shook her head and said, "Dial for me." She nodded at the phone.

"Dial?"

What was it about this group? Everyone who was supposed to be smarter than her was dumber. She waved him off and peered at the phone. Concentrating hard, she lifted the handset, and the waiter saw the light; comprehension finally descended, "Oh, dial! Yeah, dial nine and then the number."

"Thanks, bud." She brought her finger to the nine indent but had trouble finding the hole. She brought her head closer, and there - success. She tugged at 9 and listened hard. Dial tone. She dialed Fran's number. Most likely, the machine would pick up. If it did, she'd hang up, she decided.

"Hello?"

"Fran? It's me, Joey."

"Joey. It's late."

"I know. I'm sorry." Joey concentrated hard, but she found it difficult to sit up straight. Her elbow kept slipping off her knee, jerking her down. She self-corrected.

"What do you want?"

Joey frowned, unsure why she'd called, so she tried for truth. "You. I want you."

"I already said it's okay. I'm sorry about what I said about you and Mike."

"Don't be. It happened. Don't let him lie to you. He uses your apartment for shoots. He fucked me in your bed. I did it because it would be someone else if it wasn't me. This way, you can't pretend."

"Shut up, Joey."

"You know me, Fran. I don't lie about the big things. He fucked me, and he'll always fuck someone. It's who he is. He needs a new face to fuck, just 'cause he can. Find out now before you have kids. Before he breaks your heart. I'm sorry. I am. Not that I did it. I'm sorry I had to. But you're blind about him. And I love you too much to let it slide."

Silence.

"You know I love you, Fran? Fran? You there?" Joey leaned down on her long, thin thighs, trying to hear anything to show that she was not talking to the night. She thought she heard Fran breathe.

"Fuck you, Joey." The line went dead.

"Fran?" The line buzzed in her ear. "Fran?" She hung up and dialed again, very slowly. The phone rang. No answer. No machine. No Fran.

"Joey! Here you are." The jock sat on the arm of the wrought iron chaise and grinned his mindless grin. "Stan really likes you."

"Stan can go fuck himself."

The jock grinned at her. "He's pretty powerful in Hollywood. He could make you a star."

"What are you, his pimp?"

"I'm just saying." He smiled at her and reached out, rubbing her shoulders. His palm was warm, comforting.

"Where's ringlets?"

He laughed. "Audrey?" His hand made little circles against her cold back, the fingers digging into the soft flesh, feeling for the knots. She nodded, trying to keep her mind on Audrey. "Yeah, Oscar girl."

"I don't know. She's with Howard. He directed her in that movie."

Ahh, director trounced jock. So that was why he'd returned. Vaguely she was aware of the cushion next to her indenting, but the jock was kissing her, and she needed the distraction. Then she felt a hand on her breast and then hands on her everywhere all at once. She knew that Stan was there, but she couldn't figure out where the jock stopped and where Stan started.

"No."

She heard the word come out her mouth, over the soft counter-whisper of, "It's okay, you'll like it."

"No!" She struggled but got confused. There was the movement and the voices and then black. She welcomed the black.

***

Birds were tweeting. The cool light of day shuddered Joey awake. She was cold – and almost naked. Her top was gone, and her body was on display. Not covered display; revealed, exposed display. She pushed up, swallowing hard. Her mouth, filled with staleness - and something else. The bloody birds continued to twitter as she searched for her halter. She saw it on the immaculate marble floor. She stood, adjusted to the off-center world. She yanked her skirt, which had gathered at her waist, above her exposed pubis. She discovered her panties around her ankles. Her inner thighs were sticky as she smoothed down her mini. The world revolved, and she almost stumbled. *Sit down.* She plopped down on the cold cushions of the wrought iron chaise, reached for her little bit of lace, and pulled the pink undergarment in place, thinking hard. She yaw-ed out and grabbed the halter as the world tilted. With great concentration, she slipped into her halter, fumbled with the tie, and tried to remember. The bodies. Stan was there? She'd said, "No!" Hadn't she? She was sure she had. Her head throbbed. She felt tender between her legs. She instinctively placed a protective hand between her thighs. She'd definitely said, "No." The irony penetrated. When she said no, no one listened. When she told the truth, people thought it was a lie.

13

FRANNIE CHILD

Street is street and love is love. Fran went for the artistic type, everything her father was not. But fuckers come in all shapes and sizes. She wasn't sure why, but people looked at her and saw money and wheat fields. Why should she disillusion them? She came from a trailer park, and when her mother got a job, they moved to a little run-down place with three rooms. One for her, one for mom and dad, and one for the TV. Most nights, the TV room functioned as a bedroom because her dad passed out on the couch. They never woke him to get him to bed. Those were the good nights. There was a reason Fran championed the underdog. She'd watched her mother get beaten and yelled at, pushed around, anything to keep the focus off her daughter.

"Go to your room!" was shot at her often enough. *"Go to your room. Close the door. And don't come out till I say so."*

Her mom had shown her how to push the chest of drawers across the opening of the door, so she didn't have to move it too far to make it impossible for the door to open at all. Fran went to bed at night with the scuffles and the shouts. Sometimes, she sat with her hands over her ears, and sometimes, when she was younger, she played with her dolls, the fracas wafting on the currents. Desperation is a funny thing. Not funny ha-ha, but funny in the 'who would have thought' way. Men without hope come home and take out their anger on the women who love them. Men like that believe in the American way. They're the ones who sign up first when the country goes to war. They like guns, rock and roll, working in construction, and die a little each day as they realize their dreams won't come true. Their boss yells at them, the world doesn't listen to them, and the place that should make them king is a constant reminder of how nothing they tried ever came to anything.

Rich people don't know this life. Rich people have families who use their connections, so they don't struggle. They have the parachute to catch them when they fall, they have daddy pulling strings so you start out thinking you're a winner. Fran saw the people she moved with and listened to their arrogance, their complete miscomprehension of what it would be like not to have the buffer of wealth.

So, her father was the result of an uncaring world, and her mother was the butt of his anger. Fran was a calm person. She learned not to move too fast. Assess everything, don't react, and it all might ease to nothing. Her entire life had trained her to hold herself in. When Fran moved, she didn't do it in a small way. When she reacted, it was in a way that people spoke about afterward. She knew this about herself and kept that motion muffled.

When Michael came back and sweet-talked her, when he made her call Joey and apologize for accusing Joey of seducing him, the frozen hidden part of her had awakened. When Joey kept calling, she let the answering machine pick up. She wanted to believe Michael. She understood what Joey had tried to do, but she could not face the knowing in her eyes – even if it was Joey - who no one ever believed. Throw away Joey. Fran decided to throw her away, too.

Michael needed thought. She loved him - in a way. She loved his softness, the way he captured images with his camera. The way he crafted love poems for her. That he slept with Joey was not something she doubted. So why take him back? It wasn't because she was like her mother and bought into his lies. While he stood there, using his sexuality to win her over, she thought, maybe if Joey hadn't been so determined to prove him wrong, he might not have done it. There was never a reason to think he would stray, but if someone wanted you, you had to be strong to resist. She had seen

Joey in action. Fran herself had been seduced; she knew how it could happen. Joey was one of the rich people in life. She didn't value what life gave her because she had no understanding of what it was like to struggle. She took what she needed and was confident that she would get whatever she wanted. It was a life-fulfilling prophecy. Fran was still processing what had happened. It's easy for others to say, "Kick him out!" He paid half the rent; she was saving for her fashion line. Fran was practical. There were things she needed to do. So, she let him think she believed him. The call to Joey was hard. But Joey played along, both of them knowing the lie.

***

It was the second week after Fran had discovered the infidelity that Fran was in the kitchen baking and Michael entered.

"Where is my cashmere coat?"

Fran was cutting dried cherries to add to the batter. Her hand slowed to a butterfly's beat of a wing, then continued cutting.

"Fran? Do you know where my coat is?"

"Not really."

"What is that supposed to mean? Either you do, or you don't."

She turned her back to the cutting board and leaned against the counter. "Then I don't. Specifically."

He pulled a face. "I hate when you get like this. Do you know what happened to my jacket?"

She shrugged. "It was at the top of the pile I left on the east corner of the roof. I guess it blew away."

He made a hissing noise like when you shoot a dart from a tube. "Blew away?"

"Yeah. When I found out you had been cheating with Joey. Remember? I took your clothes to the four corners of the roof. It was a while before you arrived. It must've blown away."

"I thought we settled that crap about Joey."

“We did.” Fran turned back to her baking, added the yogurt to the cherry mixture. “And your coat is somewhere in Manhattan.” She stirred the batter.

You could hear the disbelief on another out-breath of air. Then silence like a statement. Fran felt her anger up a notch at his righteous indignation. She concentrated on dicing additional cherries.

“You need to replace it.” His voice was full of anger.

“No.”

“What did you say?”

“I said, ‘no.’”

“You lost my favorite coat and who knows how much else. I want it replaced.”

Fran calmly continued to chop the cherries. “There’s so much I want. God – I could be here all day listing all the things I want. Right now, I want you to think it through. Think about what you’re saying, and let me get on with my baking.”

“Fuck that.” She felt his hand on her shoulder as he dragged her around. “You—” And he stopped.

Fran was facing him with the point of the knife placed at the base of his throat. It actually touched his skin. He went to push her hand away but the look in her eyes coupled with the word, “Don’t.” Stopped him.

“Fran?”

“Now listen, don’t talk.” She spoke calmly without anger, so he understood never to manhandle her again.

He stepped back, and she stepped forward, her arm elongating to stay in contact with his flesh.

“I am not going to replace a single item that got lost. You’re not going to ask me again, and we’re not going to talk about it again. I don’t want it discussed. You fuck with me; I’ll fuck with you. You want out, then go, but you don’t stay and threaten me. I know, and you know the truth. I’m not stupid. You don’t get to tell me what to do. The next time you want to sink your dick into some pussy, just know that I know what really happened. This is the last time you ever get a second chance with me.”

He opened his mouth, and she interrupted him. “Don’t even think of calling me a name. Just shut the fuck up and go say thank you that you’re engaged to such a docile woman who loves you.”

She watched his ‘I’m-in-control-confidence’ avalanche into a panic that grew his eyes so no eyelids showed at all, and it looked like they might even pop from their sockets. She saw his mind dominate his need to run or fight as he willed himself to understand. She saw fear leak into his eyes like a cornered hen, and love was nowhere in sight.

She turned her back on that look she saw on her mother’s face a million times, focused back on her fruit, and began dicing again. Michael stood looking at her like he’d never seen her before and then slowly moved to the couch and sat staring unseeingly at the carpet. Fran combined the ingredients in the bowl and added the extra cherries. To keep from saying anything at all, she started to hum.

She poured the ingredients into the baking pan. Fran had to confront what she’d just done. Michael would never be her husband. Joey was right. He could have said “no.” It’s just one word. Fran, despite all the lessons from her childhood, had taken him back. She’d forgiven him, and begun the lie that this would be the only time he would stray. She had become her mother. Moisture splattered the batter. She felt her cheeks. She never cried. She rooted for the underdog, but she never cried, and certainly not for herself. Yet, here she was as though having hurried in from a spring shower, her cheeks unexpectedly damp. She leaned forward on straight arms like crutches supporting a broken body. How apt. She was broken. You just couldn’t tell by looking. She grabbed a handful of cookie dough and forced it into her mouth, examining the crack in the tiled countertop. In-control Frannie, out of control. Deny, deny, deny. She was familiar with the concept. She spat out the dough. Sweetness cannot dominate biliousness. She had to tell him to leave.

***

FRAN - KENTUCKY:

After I blew Daddy's face away, well, not completely, but enough, and he returned from the hospital, I'd catch him looking at me, unsure. I wasn't afraid. I'd taken him on and won. He never touched Mom again, just the one time he started yelling, and I went and stood before him and looked him dead in the eye.

"Never again. You hear." And when he opened his mouth to reply, I said, "You didn't leave the gun loaded."

I watched the knowledge and understanding trickle through his coddled brain. The disbelief, the doubt, the impossible acknowledgment that the girl he'd defended had deliberately loaded and fired, then denied, denied, denied. It was horrible to watch on his now deformed face, and I saw the pain in his eyes that his child could do that. Then the anger snapped, and a balled fist loaded to spring.

"Are you sure you want to?"

He calculated the odds, he read my intent, and lowered his fist. And they were happy, as best they could be, but he was never the same with me again. I lost my father. The air between us became blighted, and I understood how a hit could be better than nothing.

That year, I graduated high school early. The plan was to go to New York and learn Couture. It was a dream from the time I tried on my mother's ballerina dress and saw myself transformed. I would design.

The day I left, the conversations and discussions were done. Mother had encouraged me in my quest. Sewing was one of the things we did together. The whirr of the Singer Sewing machine as the needle blurred and her hand guided the material. Elvis, in the background, singing: 'Wooden Heart.' That's how I felt, like Pinocchio, wooden. I didn't want to go, but Maggievale held nothing for me. There was already a seamstress and a tailor, and dad, willing me gone.

I found him at the fence of the beaten cottage. He was leaning on the curved wood, looking at the horizon, his huge work hands clasped. His work shirt was checkered and bright against the dismal poverty of the street. He was tanned from the hours in the sun, the good side of his face visible, over his shoulder, handsome again.

"Dad."

His furrowed brow concertinaed as he decided whether to acknowledge me. He turned the ruined side of his face to me, deliberately, so that was all I saw, and no emotion could be read.

"I'm leaving now. Say goodbye to me."

He pushed away from the fence, so he half rolled to a lean and was facing me. The matador and the bull.

I almost walked away, but he spoke like he was answering an unasked question, simply, without emphasis, avoiding my gaze. "I didn't write it in my diary: fail. It wasn't my goal. It's something that infiltrates the cells, that you suck up from the ground, like a boil about to burst. You wake up, and your youth is gone. Your dreams have soured, and you're everything you swore you would never be." He was looking somewhere, but with eyes that saw inside. "You be careful, Frannie. Don't let your dreams corrode. Don't let the acid burn."

I stepped toward him, and he took me in his daddy grip, like the shooting had never happened, like the love had not run dry, like he was still my hero.

"Frannie, you are me. My seed is in you. Watch it boil and fester. See if you can keep it down." There was laughter in his voice. It was malignant, and he was joyful that his fight would be mine. "When your fury ignites, see if you can rise above it."

I moved back in his arms to see if I read his emotion clearly. I looked into the distorted face, the face that I had created, and fear gripped me that he was right. His cheek pulled up in what was now his smile, and he grabbed my face fiercely between his thumb and index finger.

"Remember your dad's advice. You're my girl: Deny, deny, deny."

I wondered if anything he said had been real, so I said what I knew to be true.

"I love you, dad. I do. I'll come by from time to time. I'll not call to let you know; I'll just come by like any child who loves her dad will do. Here's what I want you to recall at odd times when you're feeling low. If even one time I come home, and she's battered, I'll do what I started. That seed you talked about, that fury, it can be fierce, and I'll finish what I began. You know I will, and you know I can."

We stared at each other. Me, wondering if the threat was enough, him wondering – I don't know what? I kissed the lined forehead, and before I could move out of his grip, he said, "Frannie, you ever think about what happened? You even know what I did?"

I looked at him, wondering where he was headed, where his sly mind would slide.

"I did what I always told you, Frannie. When the police asked, I lied. I denied. You remember that when you think of me. I denied. And I didn't have to." He swallowed hard, and he finally looked at me honestly, and I saw love.

"Goodbye, Dad."

"Good-bye, Frannie-child."

14

BOOT SHOOT

The House of Rest was restful but wrong. *"I'm not manic depressive."* Joey thought as she got ready for her Boot Shoot fashion shoot. Boot Shoot was an up-and-coming company that dressed teenagers like they were 50's movie stars. The ads featured breasts first and foremost. Kohled eyes and big pouty mouths, like Bridget Bardot in *And God Created Woman.* Belly buttons and super long legs teamed with cowboy boots. Cowboy hats were a favorite too, and long hair, usually blown across parted lips and sticking to bulging boobs. Joey was in the make-up chair as the huge Velcro rollers were placed in her platinum hair. On a table lay hair pieces, which would be added for fullness, and then a fan would be set up off-camera to create the wind. A lanky boy, all pecs and lips and cheekbones, flirted with the photographer. Joey wondered if he'd had to go down on Gie to get the work. It wasn't that he wasn't beautiful, just that the agencies were full of beautiful boys and these days guys had to trade sex as much as the girls did.

"Open your mouth, Sweetie," the make-up artist ordered applying another layer of liquid lust. "Okay. Chin down, let's see."

Joey lowered her chin.

"Have you been drinking enough water? Your skin looks a little dry?"

Joey resisted the urge to retaliate. "You sure know how to make a girl feel good." She laughed it off, not letting the casual put-downs that are part of a modeling gig get to her this time, but then a voice floated to her.

"Darling, don't pull that face. It shows your lines."

Bitch! There's a difference between thoughtless stupidity and just plain vindictiveness, and as Joey was an expert in the latter, she recognized it immediately. Without turning she glanced over her shoulder and met the gaze of Cara, dismissively. "Hmmm? Really? What do you use on your top lip? For those lines when you pout? Maybe you should try something different? Do they show up in shots yet?"

She pretended to dust off a hair from her face. Nonchalant. That was the key. Never let them see that their words had an effect. That was the killer. She knew that from school. The moment they sensed weakness, they'd come in for the kill. Well, she wasn't that kid trying to please anymore. She'd developed armor, and if need be, she had the weapons to wound.

She understood Cara's fear. Cara had been the Boot Shoot girl for two years and wasn't ready to be replaced. This is the way it worked. They tried out a new girl as a 'second,' and if she had 'it' – the company had a new face.

Boot Shoot, or BS, as the brand was known on the street, was a star maker. Cara looked at Joey and knew she had what it took to make Cara yesterday's news. She wasn't ready to go. Joey slipped from her chair and loped over to the bathroom. Once inside, she examined her face. Without the Thorazine and lithium, she 'felt' again. She didn't think she was cresting the highs and lows that she had in Europe. It didn't take a manic depressive to wig out with what Giovanni had done to her. Sometimes, people do crazy things because they are driven to them in an act of desperation. Crazy was sometimes the normal thing to do. She knew she wasn't manic-depressive. She just felt too much and needed things people never thought to offer – sympathy, attention, and love. She examined her ass in the mirror. Had she gained weight? She couldn't tell. She searched her purse. She could do with a hit. She felt the darkness beckon, the sadness seep in. Panic took her by the throat. She didn't want to slide into the black hole again. Whatever happened on the terrace at the Alzheimer's event had not been forgotten. She wasn't going to make a pun about Alzheimer's and remembering what had gone down on the black and white patio. It was scary shit. She never wanted that to happen again. She pushed down on the feeling of acting out. To do something wild to show she didn't care. She cared. She didn't want to be used anymore, with her consent or without it. She needed to change. Huge eyes swallowed her face in the mirror. She closed her eyes. *Shake it off. Smile!* Her eyes stayed shut. *Smile! Laugh! Be casual!*

The small space of the single bathroom, painted black, pushed in on her. She had to get out. She flung open the door to be confronted by a man in jeans and a billowing shirt. He looked uncomfortable in his clothes, and since the clothes were BS – that took some doing.

Neither moved, each waiting for the other to say something or get out of the way. When nothing happened, each spoke simultaneously—then stopped. They laughed. His teeth overlapped. Joey focused on the mouth. When you model, everyone is perfect, and if they aren't, they get themselves fixed. Editors pulled you apart as though you were deaf, so everyone worked really hard to avoid the poison darts that dripped from lips and stripped the target of their already weakened confidence. Even the people behind the lights put themselves together in such a way that you noticed them for their uniqueness. Cachet, everyone associated with making the photograph perfect became perfect by association. Now, here was a man who had not made the effort to be perfect. In her world, imperfection was interesting.

"Maybe I should let you exit the bathroom before I introduce myself?" The overlapping teeth made his lips part in interesting ways as he spoke; he sounded like James Earl Jones, with a hint of foreign. His voice made her feel safe.

"Hey, it's where all the cool people meet these days." She stepped out of the bathroom. "You need to go, or do you just have a thing for hanging outside the john?"

His eyes flitted to the left, trying to figure out a reply.

"Pervert," she shot and watched the consternation cross his face, so she took pity on him. She moved in close, "I'm messing with you, but that's your name now – Perv."

She went over to the rack and started flicking through the clothes while Cara cooed, "Christian, how was Bali?"

"Good."

"I'm still mad at you for not taking me with you."

"It wasn't a luxury trip."

"Sure, lying on the beach is always tough."

"I was documenting the effect of plastics on the indigenous people." He sounded embarrassed and a little exasperated.

"How come?" asked Joey over her shoulder, genuinely curious.

"Short version? Western multinationals tend to make third-world nations and emerging markets dependent rather than self-sufficient. I'm part of a philanthropic organization trying to counter that."

Ahhh, that made sense. He had to be connected to some charity that was doing a cross-promotion with BS. It was unusual to see a person of color at a modeling shoot. Beverly Johnson had made history by becoming the first black woman to appear on *Vogue* back in '74. The Brits had done it in '66 with Donyale Luna, but integration had not become a thing. Bethann Hardison had taken her minute of fame and held up a mirror to the bias in the industry. She had started her own agency and was advocating for inclusion. None of that explained why he was at the shoot.

"Okay. Philanthropy. But what's that got to do with plastics or BS?"

"Plastics are like diamonds – they last forever. They get pulled by the world's currents and wash up on beaches, create islands of waste, and interfere with the local's ability to fish. A group of us are trying to bring awareness. You know. Change the tide?"

"Cool." Joey looked at him with interest. He registered her attention and his face infused. Had he blushed? Joey frowned. The last time she saw anyone blush it was the South African back in

Hamburg, now, here was a guy with obvious clout, doing the same thing – like being looked at made him awkward? Weird.

"Are we going to keep any of these?" Cara's voice interrupted, oblivious to the charge between Joey and Christian but maybe insinuating calculatedly.

Cara caressed a wife-beater in baby pink adorned with long leather strips. Joey examined the man with the crooked teeth who was suddenly avoiding her gaze.

"Sure," he replied to Cara, his eyes on the clothes laid out for the shoot. "Speak to Hillary. She's handling the merchandise." His eyes darted to Joey. Again, the infusion when their eyes met. He wiped his brow as his face sheened. "You want to choose something?"

"Who are you?"

"Christian Addea," he said like she should know.

"That explains everything." She shrugged, obviously clueless, and moved to the cool boots spread out on a blanket with the rest of the BS clothes that they would use in the shoot. Christian hovered as Joey lowered herself to touch the soft suede boots. Did she want them? Not really. She stood, and they found themselves too close, but neither moved.

"You're Joey," he stated the obvious. "We met before." Joey stared at him blankly. "On First Avenue, maybe three months ago?"

Joey vaguely recalled the disembodied feeling of her first day back in Manhattan, remembering her need to be touched.

"I asked you out for a drink – at like ten in the morning." Christian blushed again.

"You obviously knew my reputation."

"No, I just didn't know what to say."

She laughed. "And you're connected to BS, how?"

There was a surprised silence, then he said with a shrug, "I own the company."

"You?"

"Yeah."

Joey thought about what she knew about BS. Not much.

"Surprised because I'm black?"

The thought never occurred to her. She pulled a face. "What's that got to do with it? Nah, I just thought John Welsh headed it up."

"He's the front man. I'm the business end." As a way to bypass his suggestion, he elaborated, "We started the line on the side in school. John's mother came up with the designs; John – how should I put it – propagated the line. John was cool, and I noticed how everyone wanted what he had. It was my idea to sell it to them. I'd always had a summer job as a camp counselor, whatever, so I had some money for a few one-offs. My parents are immigrants from Ghana. You know immigrants…."

"Not really."

"It was rhetorical. We work hard and save everything. Never know when you have to pick up and leave. So I had a little cash. My parents believed in me. They invested. I handled the overhead and made sure we used most of the money to generate the next hot thing while still having a little to play with. We began with leather wrist bands for guys, but soon discovered that girls were willing to shell out money more often and for variations of a theme."

Joey listened, noting how his words tumbled out when he was comfortable. He had one hand jammed in the pocket of his trousers; the other unconsciously played with the gold cross on a chain visible through his unbuttoned sky-blue BS shirt. She could almost see him as a kid, seeing an opportunity and jumping in.

"It's a good combo. John likes the flash, and I like being behind the scenes." Joey looked around. "He's not here. We usually don't do the shoots. Just sometimes."

He looked embarrassed again.

"Like if you're in Bali," she teased.

"No, we did a shoot at one of our houses, then I went on alone. The plastics in the water, it's becoming a thing. I'm – we, we're trying to help out. I don't…. I'm not the glamour side."

"Yeah, you already said. That's why you're here, right?" She smiled the challenge, and he blushed again. "So you're a do-gooder. Think you can make a difference?"

"Never know until you try."

"Why do you care?"

A little frown creased between his black brows. "Someone has to."

"Point is, most don't." Again, the disappointment in his eyes.

Joey felt the sudden urge to do the unexpected, to explain herself. "I'm just saying. I've done the whole philanthropic crowd thing and it's all about pictures in the paper and branding a product. From what I figure, once overhead and promotional costs are taken, where's the profit? Why make the party, why not just give if you're going to…." She let the words trail. "You seem to really want to make a difference, but you also said you're not into the glamour, yet you were on the other shoot; now here you are again. I just tend to pick up on bullshit. If I do, I call it out or ask about it. But I don't know you, so I guess I don't give a shit." She smiled a cover girl smile at him to take the sting out of the words. Who gives a fuck? She thought: *Let him fire me*. "Anyway, the owner of the company has a right to be wherever he wants to be – just usually, they're not at fashion shoots." She crossed to the photographer. "How long before we start?"

"We're ready to rock 'n roll."

The lights were focused on the circular stairs of Spanish wrought iron. The three models changed and arranged themselves in front of the camera. "Cara, I want you sitting. Joey, back to the camera standing, Raoul sideways between them," Gui called the shots, snapping Polaroids.

Christian peered over his shoulder and whispered to Gui.

The photographer walked to the threesome. "Actually, Joey, you and Cara switch places. Cara, let's show off that back. Joey, face the camera."

***

Joey knew that Christian felt a bond with her. She just didn't feel one back. Joey was starting her life over again. She could be the BS girl. She knew it just as surely as she knew Michael would screw around on Fran. Should she smile, maybe flirt a little? Do something to make this man believe that she wanted him? She's done it before and more.

***

HAMBURG 1976:

In Hamburg, all the models from the Pension Haben went on a go-see. It was for a new make-up line that the Pharmaceutical giant Dep-Star was introducing. Joey was already burning up the fashion trail with her wild eyes and her woman expression on a post-pubescent girl frame. She felt confident she could blow the others out of the water - that the contract was hers. She chose to go in last. It was dark outside. Inside the interview room, the naked yellow light reflected off the semi-gloss white walls. Fran was in Italy shooting a *Vogue* layout. Tara Bean had been the first in the pod from their agency to be seen. Roma and Charlie had gone in half an hour before and were waiting for her so they could leave together. Joey deliberately arrived an hour late, and even then, the crowd had barely thinned, but she was the last to sign in, just as she had planned.

She slunk into the room. Pieter Weiner, the photographer who would do the layout, was in his late thirties. His name was well known. It was a surprise that he'd chosen such a seedy location to hold the go-sees. Usually, the photographers starting out were located in the red light district. They were as poor and as desperate as the girls they shot. The successful photographers had huge studios with lighting equipment and backdrops at the ready. Their addresses reflected their success.

Weiner flipped through her book, pausing to linger on the photo of her arched in the bronze sunset, a white mesh bikini wet against her body, her blonde hair slicked. Next to it was a photo taken on the same shoot, but a close-up. Her eyes were surrounded with greasy black make-up, her mouth huge, painted neutral, slightly parted, showing her white teeth - her pink tongue peeking through. They had placed grains of sand on the curve of her cheekbone and the crest of her lip. The light hair and eyes against the deep tan and pink tongue were sensual.

His hands went inside his trousers, and he adjusted himself discretely before flipping through the rest of the pictures quickly.

"Thank you."

She expected more. "You liked them?"

He prevaricated. "You have a good book."

"Will I get the contract?"

He pulled a face, noncommittal, but it didn't look good. "I liked the first girl."

"Tara?" she asked in disbelief.

He flipped through the cards of the models he saw all day and sure enough in the short pile, right on top, was Tara's card.

"And the other one." He pulled out Charlie's card. "They have breasts."

"It's for a make-up line," said Joey. "Anyway, I have breasts."

He made the not-so-sure expression again.

"This is bullshit." She stood, lifted her T-shirt, braless underneath. "Nothing wrong with my breasts."

"Theirs are fuller," he said. "I don't know how yours will photograph."

She pulled down her shirt, reached for her book, and just as she stalked to the door, he said, "Maybe you should do a test."

She turned to him. "When?"

The scrunched-up face thing again. "I fly to Berlin tomorrow to meet with the executives and tell them who I want to work with."

"What about now?" she asked.

"I suppose I could take some Polaroids." His eyes moved back to Charlie's card. "Her breasts were the best."

"Take the shots now," said Joey. "My friends are outside waiting for me. I'll tell them to go. We can do some poses, maybe like you would shoot the campaign, just to see?"

He shrugged. "Why not?"

Joey found Charlie and Roma and told them to leave without her. "Pieter Weiner wants to do a test with me." She saw the hope fade from Roma and Charlie's eyes. Pieter Weiner didn't want to test them; Joey must be the front-runner. They smiled, wished her luck, and left. Pieter taped a handwritten sign to the door: Interviews Closed.

Pieter Weiner had grabbed a bottle from somewhere and he now poured two shots into Styrofoam cups. He spoke of working with the top girls and how each of them did something for someone to get ahead. "Hamburg is full of pretty, long-legged girls…. How do you think Veronique got to where she is?"

Veronique was the current 'it' girl. She was everywhere and on everything. She was on her way to America to make her millions.

"Let me tell you a story," said Pieter, topping up her cup. "Veronique was nothing until Jacques started pushing her. She couldn't get hired. I turned her away myself. She has no tits. But her nipples - they're huge, like little tits themselves. As if the nipples compensated for their lack of breasts. Her nipples were like little penises. Always pushing up against her shirt. Jacques, he's an ass man, and he likes big nipples. So he tells her, one day, you let me fuck your ass, and I'll give you a chance. It was for a campaign like the one you are here for. A campaign that could make or break a girl's career. Veronique, she's smart. She says, 'Okay.' She lets him fuck her ass, and she gets the campaign. You understand what I'm saying?" he asked. "You know? You give a little to get a little. Or, in this case, a lot."

Joey understood exactly. There was a price.

"Take off your top. Rub your breasts so your nipples get hard," he commanded.

Joey complied.

"Good. Now get down on your knees."

Two weeks later, Joey casually asked her agent if they'd heard who got the campaign. She got the reply that the entire set-up had been a hoax. The man who interviewed all the girls was not Pieter Weiner. He was an imposter. A down-and-out loser who had pulled the stunt before. The police had him in custody for false impersonation.

"Why do these men do it?" asked the booker. "I don't know what they get out of it." Joey had shrugged, remembering the pungent smell and the feel of those grubby hands on her.

***

NEW YORK CITY:

There are some things you never forget. Even though the man with the crooked teeth seemed like he was different, she wasn't the same girl from Hamburg anymore. The House of Rest had changed her. The night on the patio changed her even more. She was on some kind of journey. Things were stirring up. The old behaviors didn't work anymore. Fran proved that. Even if sleeping with Michael was a 'Joey-pre-House-of-Rest-action,' it was done for the right reasons. If only Fran would acknowledge that truth. Joey rubbed her earlobe like she did when she was thinking. No, she wasn't going to pretend. She was going to try and be Joey – whatever that meant - and see if she was enough.

15

CONFESSIONS

"You're like a crab that lost its shell with your overlapping smile and your good boy causes." She flashed her cover girl smile.

She knew the words challenged Christian in a way that powerful men found provocative. His awkwardness, whenever he caught her eye, prompted her to play with him like he was a labrador pup. The banter was like a ball he could chase. She needed lightness. She wasn't going to fuck him to get the job. For all his success, he seemed - sweet. "Mr. I-Feel-Your-Pain." A laugh gurgled out, watching him try to figure out the correct response. She knew she could have him without any effort at all, but just because she could didn't mean she should. Joey registered the choice and felt a flare of pride that she might be starting to make better choices.

"You're lucky you're meeting me now, 'cause before, I'd destroy someone like you." She grinned, running her tongue beneath her teeth, reflective and a little in awe of her growth.

Despite her put-down of his philanthropic methods earlier, or maybe because of it, Christian had stayed close throughout the shoot. He talked to her as a person rather than a thing. And somehow, maybe because of the manner in which he spoke to her, even though she was determined not to, she agreed to coffee with him after the shoot. She could see why he was successful. He was focused and not easily deflected; but he was business, not life-savvy, and easy to shock. She'd known a lot of Christians in her life; she could use him if she wanted, without any effort. She knew what to say to hook him, what to do to keep him. She was almost tempted, just for the distraction it would provide. If she was honest, it was good to talk and have someone actually listen. She'd had no one to talk to since the House of Rest. Plus, he talked about things no one else talked to Joey about – like she had a brain and her opinion was valued.

His brow creased at her words, his grin revealing his crowded teeth. He spoke like Clint Eastwood in *Dirty Harry*, like his teeth were glued together. "Destroy is a pretty strong word."

"Not deliberately destroy – well, maybe – sometimes." She laughed. Then frowned at the confession.

Why was she saying these things to him? Something had happened to her. A lot of things. But Fran, and Michael, and the assault on the penthouse patio, and – maybe The House of Rest.... Fucking with people because she could, now felt like a pointless game.

"Honestly? I don't know how it happens. Maybe just as a consequence of – association – but it happens." She was still smiling, but not in her eyes. "Be around me long enough and you'll get burnt, y'know?" She met his gaze. "But – that was before." She looked out the window. "I'm – I'm trying to change."

Joey was tired. She reminded herself of her promise to stay straight for a while. She wanted to stop the chaos, but she didn't really know how. She knew he was sniffing around. He seemed nice. So, she figured she'd better prepare him, so he didn't become another wreck left in her jet stream. She felt weighed down by her past. Honesty was awkward.

He deflected her alerts. "Good. Change if you want to. I kind of like you the way you are. Anyway, you've got me figured wrong. I'm not that easy to crush. You don't become head of a company our size without being tough. I'm first generation American. I know how it feels to not be taken seriously, to be judged on my outsides. Really. I *do* feel your pain, but my shell is intact. I'm not easily damaged."

Joey thought of Fran and Giovanni; was it her shell or theirs that gotten broken? She grew annoyed at his dismissal of something she had tried so hard to convey. “Look, I’m not denying your truth, but are you hearing mine? This isn’t about you. I’ve got patterns I’m beginning to see. In my life, I destroy or get destroyed. I don’t mean to – it just happens. I find myself amongst the slithers of glass having impaled someone or bleeding myself. I never used to be able to put it into words but I’m finally – seeing a pattern.”

“Amongst the slivers of glass? Impaled?” He questioned her words with humor. She held his gaze, and when she didn’t smile back, he became interested in the saltshaker and moved it like a chess piece. When she didn’t retract her words, it became his turn to apologize. “I didn’t mean to undermine your words. My advice? If you see it, you can stop it.”

“Can I?”

“Yes.”

“I’m not so sure. I have loved someone for a while – years. You know how I loved them?”

“You love someone?” He glanced away.

“Yeah, someone who has been kind to me; always.”

“Why wouldn’t they?”

“I’m not easy to be kind to. I’m not used to kind. Kind doesn’t happen very often and when it does, I get confused.”

“Seriously?” The tone incongruous. “Joey, super model, that the world wants to please, is unused to kind? Seems unlikely.”

“I slept with a friend’s fiancé.”

She felt like he was her confessor. The more he explained away her logic the more invested she got in getting him to see beyond the public projection. Usually, she let people make their own conclusions about her. Usually, they were so totally wrong. Usually, she didn’t give a fuck what they thought. So why was she working so hard to get this do-gooder to see her truth?

He assessed her without expression, like Sidney Poitier looked at his students in *To Sir, With Love,* that she'd watched on Turner Classics at The House of Rest.

God, I miss The House of Rest.

The thought came to her and surprised her. Maybe she was projecting the role of her psychiatrist, Dr. Brand, onto Christian? Saying the things she wouldn't say at The House of Rest to this man who was determined to think the best of her?

She added another confession. "I did it deliberately 'cause I knew he was incapable of fidelity."

"Was that your point to prove?" That stopped her.

"Someone had to."

"Why?"

She laughed. "See. *That's* important. Why? No one else wants to know 'why' about me, ever. They draw their conclusions and they're never right."

"So? Explain it to me."

"It's complicated."

"If you did it deliberately, I figure it has to be."

"When I first got to New York her fiancé and I, we used each other."

"Used?"

"Yeah. You said you wanted the truth. Here it is. I didn't love him or want him, but we had sex – lots of it." Again, he squirmed, not sure he wanted to hear what he had asked to be revealed. "He was with someone, some girl who believed in him. He needs people to take care of him, mother him. I'm never that girl. So he played at domesticity, but he'd steal away with me to – what should I call it – the high life, fast track, all the clichés. He lived that with me and others. I knew it. Didn't really care. It was an understanding. He was – you know how you hang with people and have easy, fun times with them, and things happen? You don't count on them, but it's easy and fast?"

"Not really."

"Well, where have you been? Everyone does it."

"Not me."

"Well, I guess you're special."

"I guess I am."

"Well, he isn't and that's my point. When I'm with someone, I'm with them and when I'm not, I'm nailing the nail-able." Off his look. "I'm trying to change."

Again, the polite bob of his head. She saw his desire slipping away like blood from a wound, but he didn't stop her, and he didn't move away. She stayed with the truth, like he was a benign inquisitor, prompting admissions and links she had barely crystalized even to herself, with his silent chocolate gaze.

"Go on." He encouraged when she lapsed into silence.

She shrugged. The need to explain expunged.

"Say it all," Christian prompted; the words gave her permission.

"This way, that way. I knew Mike. Had seen enough of him to understand that he plays both sides of the world. He always went back to Alice, his girl, y'know? We'd do stuff outside the borders. Some things I saw him do I would never do myself, then he'd go back and pretend he was this straight arrow. Everyone knew, and in the end even she knew, and it destroyed her. She wasn't a friend, and I did nothing that he wasn't doing with everyone else. We kind of let her pretend that he was what she thought he was, but how could he be? The pretense got too big for her. It got ugly in all the predictable ways, and we laughed about it. Anticipated it. And when it happened, we didn't think of her. We celebrated him for getting her to stick around as long as she did. Then I get back to New York and I hear he's changed, he's gone straight and his new girl is my friend; incapable of hurting anyone. I've never seen her do a bad thing ever – and, he gave me reason to suspect he hadn't changed at all. It got to where I just couldn't see her married to this guy, 'cause I *knew* he hadn't changed."

"Maybe he had."

"If he had he would've said 'no.' I've said no. Not often, but I've said it. Bet you say no a lot."

"Yes."

"I knew that."

"So did you explain 'why' to your friend?"

"She won't talk to me."

"That makes things tricky."

Joey fingered the cutlery on the fine linen, oblivious to the restaurant's cacophony.

"That does make things 'tricky.'" She admitted, twisting the word out, but she couldn't hold up the sarcasm now that she finally had someone to examine the nuances with. "I hadn't anticipated that. Gratitude, sure, but to be deleted, amputated from her life? Never occurred to me." She flashed an empty smile. "Tricky, indeed." She looked out the restaurant's window again, acknowledging the understatement. "Tricky." She frowned. "You talk like an English schoolgirl. Or maybe it's 'cos you're foreign."

"I think you're confused. I'm American. I'm black. I'm a man. This is how I speak."

"Yeah, but still like an English schoolgirl." She laughed, trying to lighten the mood.

"And you speak like a truck driver."

"It's not the first time I've heard that." A genuine smile, then. "So, Mr. Crooked Teeth. I'm not dating material. Don't get to know me. You won't like me at all."

"What's your friend's name?"

"Fran. Fran Childres. Whatever. It's done. I'm used to walking away from people I love."

He narrowed his eyes, gave a wry smile. "I can't figure out if you're for real or you just speak like this for effect."

She looked him in the eye. What did she have to say for him to believe her? She was tired of pretend. Of not being heard. Of keeping things hidden. Of not being believed. She took a breath. "I gave away my baby."

***

CHRISTIAN:

The words were whispered like one said something mundane, that no one doubted. Like the confession was unremarkable. Delivered with less emphases than you'd announce a sale at Sachs. Then they just hung there. She said it so casually that he knew it was true, but he asked, "What was that?"

She pulled in her lips so it looked like she had no mouth and she shut her eyes really tight. Then she smiled and said, "Nothing."

Christian berated himself for playing for time, for pretending not to hear what he heard.

"Did you say?"

Joey tossed her napkin on the table. "I'm done. I can't do this." She grabbed her bag and pushed herself away from the table. "I'm outta here."

He stood a second too late. He tried to follow, but the waitress ran after him with the bill. He flipped open his wallet, but the hundred dollar bills he had that morning were gone, probably lifted on the photoshoot. "I'll be right back," he assured the girl.

"Sorry sir, you need to take care of the bill first." She widened her stance like he might bolt.

"I'm trustworthy. If I say I'll be back, I'll be back."

The waitress gave him a blank stare – she'd most likely heard that a thousand times. "Sorry sir, restaurant policy."

"Here, take my credit card. I'll return to sign it."

"Sorry sir, I need you to sign it first before you leave, and we'll need some ID, too."

"Goddammit." He waited impatiently as she processed the credit card. He signed it, flashed his driver's license, and waited as she meticulously compared the signatures.

"Thank you, sir, and have a nice day."

He hurried into the street. Joey was gone.

***

JOEY:

Joey had never told anyone. Never said the words before. Not even to Fran. So why him? Why now? Since the House of Rest, something had begun to happen. The techniques taught to question and acknowledge had penetrated her reactions, so at night, she'd think back on her day and ask why. Why did I do that? Recently, her answers seemed unreasonable. She had gone through life as though she was compelled. Now Joey realized there were choices and options. Most people did not react first and think later. Joey had been thinking since she was tossed away by Fran, and the answers were coming fast and furiously. She couldn't figure out how all the puzzle parts connected. People looked at her; they never listened to her. She found a desire to talk, and the crooked-toothed man, Christian, was the first one who wanted to hear.

She needed to see Fran.

16

RED LICORICE

Joey was walking on Central Park East, close to the zoo, when she was surrounded by little girls holding hands. They wore dark blue cardigans on top of white shirts with Peter Pan collars. Wide-brimmed hats adorned their heads. Their shoes, shiny Mary Janes. The expanse of legs between their anklets and the bottom of their grey skirts varied. She slowed down and then stopped amidst them. An oak surrounded by saplings. A harried supervisor tried her best, 'listen-to-me' voice. "Girls. Girls! Move to the left. *My* left. We're blocking the sidewalk. Girls!" Joey in the midst of giggles and murmurs.

"We're going to the zoo." Piped up a little girl with blonde pigtails.

"Are you?" Joey's unsure around children.

"I'm going to see the Panda bear. It lives in the Arctic," added the chatty child.

"But this *isn't* the Arctic," said a second little girl, holding the first one's hand. The kids have been paired off. The knowledgeable one wears glasses. Her braided hair tied with precise navy bows. Her lips pouted over gapped teeth.

"I didn't say it was." The blonde was defensive. She was only 8 but they'd already pegged her as dumb. The brunette rolled her eyes at Joey.

"A zoo represents all of the different animals of the world; only this zoo is too small to hold too many."

"Have you been to the Arctic?" asked the blonde, trying to get the attention back.

"Don't be idiotic," interrupted the brunette. "No one goes to the Arctic. It's too cold."

The brunette, like most of the non-blondes Joey knew, carried a supercilious attitude, like they were better than blondes. Just because men prefer blondes and brunettes never get noticed, brunettes think it's okay to talk down to blondes. Joey was familiar with condescension. So, for the sake of little blonde girls everywhere, she decided to take on Miss Smarty-pants.

"Actually, people do go to the Arctic," she stated. As a grown-up, she naturally had first dibs on the IQ chain. "You should ask your mummy to research it for you."

"We watch the Discovery channel," informed the brunette, like that gave her superior information. The little blonde watched the back and forth like a spectator at a tennis match. Her eyes settled on Joey. She was rooting for her.

"Good for you." Joey turned back to the blonde. "I have visited the Arctic. I conducted experiments there."

The brunette looked doubtful. "Are you a scientist?"

"Yes, I am."

She looked Joey up and down - the YSL mini skirt, the Thierry Mugler suede boots, the padded shoulder leather jacket. "You don't look like a scientist."

"What does a scientist look like?" asked Joey. The brunette screwed up her face to think about it. "You shouldn't be prejudiced. You should get your mummy to look up the word 'prejudice' in the dictionary for you. You shouldn't judge people on how they look. It's not nice."

The brunette juts out her jaw, but she's not through with Joey yet.

"What kind of experiments did you do?"

"We tested to see how long little girls could stay out in the cold without anything warm on." Joey didn't miss a beat. "We had to use several little girls. Mainly nasty ones who made others feel bad. Do you know the kind? Those who never shut up and are mean to everyone else. Know-it-alls."

The brunette's face flushed. "Miss?" she yelled. "Miss!"

The blonde smiled conspiratorially at Joey, who winked at the kid. The child dug in her pocket and offered Joey a twirl of red licorice. Joey flushed. She didn't want to touch that licorice, but she could tell it was important to the blonde. Joey suddenly thought of Goldie, her daughter, giving licorice to some stranger, and how she would want that stranger to react. She struggled to breathe like someone was pushing down on her chest. "Thank you." She took the licorice. The woman in front waved her arm, and the entire group of little girls moved forward. Joey felt empty. She stood clutching the red licorice, the sole oak after a forest fire.

***

1973:

Joey was out at the pool with her friends. Jane pulled out a pack of red licorice, Joey's favorite. They were lying in the sun, long skinny legs like wet spaghetti, gangly and unformed but hinting at the beauty to come. She was halfway through the swirl of licorice when she felt the biliousness rise. She threw up right there next to the chaise lounge while her friends 'eewed' and ran for her mother.

Mother arrived, attempting to hide the effect of several martinis. "Josaphina. Why didn't you go to the bathroom?"

Kids are like criminals when the police turn up, they scatter at any sign of trouble. Not that Joey remembered them leaving with her face stuck in the toilet. Then five minutes later, she was fine. Like nothing happened. Still, she always associated what happened afterward with red licorice.

Throughout the beginning of that summer, she threw up randomly. She was also gaining weight. Not much. Her hips filling out, her breasts getting bigger. Boy, were they ever huge? It made her look older than her fourteen years. Mother chalked it up to puberty.

Three months earlier, her period had arrived in a gush while she was having lunch at the club. Mother's current boyfriend was with them. He wasn't that happy when mother kept saying that her little girl was all grown up and no longer a baby. She drank a toast to it. Mother was never the nurturing kind. After Daddy died, Mother only focused on two things: the bottle and her revolving door of men. The current one had lasted the longest. Joey liked him the least. Since Daddy died, she didn't really have an escape, no alone time. The bizarre trio did everything together until Mother would fall asleep in a drunken stupor, and then it was just the suitor and Joey.

After six weeks of throwing up, the nausea just vanished. Joey was tired a lot, and whereas the red licorice had made her toss her lunch before, she now seemed to live off it. Packets were devoured in secret because mother insisted that Joey's widening girth was due to a poor diet.

Every August she went for her annual check-up. When the doctor examined her, he asked, "Did you get your period yet, Josaphina?"

"Yeah, but just for one month, and then it went away."

He looked at her gravely. "Lie down." His hands flew over her stomach, down toward her pelvis.

She looked to the side and hummed so she couldn't be aware of where his hands were.

"Do you have a boyfriend?" he asked.

She shook her head.

"You can tell me."

"I don't. Ask mother."

He pursed his lips. "You are sexually active, aren't you?"

She could feel her cheeks getting red. "No! Why would you say that?"

"Because unless I'm very wrong, you are pregnant."

"How?"

"Sex," he said sarcastically, then off her look of utter embarrassment, "Hasn't anyone spoken to you about sex?"

Joey shook her head.

“You know, sometimes just fooling around, it’s rare, but it can happen that….”

“No. That’s not how it happened.” Joey had to think. “Don’t tell mother.” That was urgent.

“I have to.”

“She’ll send me away.”

“No. She won’t.” He smiled a gentle, sad smile. “Look, there are some things we can do. First, let me run some tests to find out how far along you are. Then we’ll talk again.”

***

She clamped her lips on the scream, and the pain passed. Monitors beeped. Brisk people in ugly pastel uniforms scurried confidently. She would jettison the burden. That’s what she’d been dreaming of for the six months since the discovery.

The scenes that followed the discovery were her daytime nightmares, refusing to fade, drilled into the new granite of her emotion: The inquisition, the pressure to name some kid as the spoiler of her virtue. The complete refusal to acknowledge her Mother’s beau was the culprit. Her mother’s anger when he’d left. The recrimination of how Joey had Lolita’d him into it. The slurred words pounding home the fact that it had to be Joey’s fault because mother would never let a pedophile into her house.

Joey was four months along when the pregnancy was discovered, so abortion was a questionable option. Yet her mother pushed for it. It was the OB-GYNs who refused, their Park Avenue offices, faux libraries where people with incubating babies read magazines like *Mother*, *Parents*, and *The Fetus Inside*. But once you got past that civilized gentility, you were in a room with metal stirrups and machines. Where men stuck things between your legs, just the way it had happened in the semi-darkness of her room. Eventually, they went to Queens and a waiting room where there was no pretense.

Her mother threw many tantrums in the hour they'd waited but stopped when the emaciated teenager in the corner grabbed her flat stomach, groaning, blood seeping into her skirt, staining her pale legs ink red in a pattern the rain makes on a windowpane when it's storming, and you're watching for your father's car to arrive, not yet knowing it never will. In the silence that ate up the stuffy room, crowded with anxious women, no one's gaze connecting, the scratchy updates of Richard Nixon's impeachment became a welcome distraction. Not because of the politics – what did a few lies matter compared to what they were about to do, compared with the convoluted scenarios they created to fortress their reputation from the truth? It was just good to know that no one was pure, not even the President of the greatest country in the world.

"Come!" her Mother spoke with the urgency reserved for words like FIRE or HELP. Hiding beneath her sunglasses, her color like rancid cream, Joey's mother clutched her water bottle drained of the Vodka she'd filled it with in order to face this excursion into the land of never-happened, her Valentino suit contrasting with the dirty room.

"But…"

"We're leaving," she interrupted with the confidence of a woman accustomed to being obeyed. "Now, Josaphina!"

With the abortion off the table, a sick sister was created. The plan was this: Joey's mother, who had never cared for anything, needed to depart to care for her sibling, and Josaphina would leave school to help. Their conspiracy drew them together for the first time in years; their common cause, that no one they knew would know about her pregnancy, ever.

Sequestered away from their Connecticut connections, Joey and her mother stayed in a beach house on the Isle of Palms in South Carolina. Joey was tutored while her mother swung in a hammock, listening to the palmetto bugs, and slapped at the creative mosquitoes that penetrated the protective netting. Besides the tutor and the OB-GYN, it was just mother and Joey. For the first time since the column of beau's had begun, Mother was manless, and Joey understood how much it cost her to remain that way.

Mother hired a pale-yellow Cadillac convertible and a driver to get to the pre-natal visits. In complete silence, with the cloying air curling mother's straightened hair, they traversed the long rides to Charleston across the Cooper River Bridge, seated together on the back seat, each looking their separate ways. Sometimes, the songs on the radio would play like themes to their lives. Barbra Streisand's 'The Way We Were,' or Dionne Warwick and the Spinners' 'And Then Came You,' before her mother made the driver turn the radio off. Silence became safer. Life leaked away. Joey kept her mind in a box, but her body needed an escape. She started sneaking vodka when her mother passed out. The last month found them making the trip weekly, despite the heat, Joey dressed in a Jackie O A-line coat to hide her size.

And then the moment. Joey couldn't keep the contractions at bay; this thing created in pain and guilt would be born that same way. She swiveled her gaze through the fog of the epidural, fastening on Mother's face. There was something in her eyes – or maybe she was sober.

The doctor said, "Push."

Joey bore down. Her vagina tore as she unleashed a scream, and her daughter was born.

Joey thought she heard her mother whisper, "Forgive me." But she couldn't be sure.

***

GOLDIE:

The baby was placed in Joey's arms. A girl. Her eyes shut like a drowned rat, her pale hair plastered against her crown, her face pink. Joey felt no connection with this child. Then the girl, her baby, clasped her finger. The grip was so strong. Joey felt something deep inside her tighten like all the wickedness that had filtered into her life was squeezed out. A fierce possessiveness in its place. This was her child. She was a mother. She bent her cheek to this pink, slightly damp arc that had been growing in her belly, the creature she had created and carried. Joey believed she smelled like heaven. Possessiveness replaced by protectiveness. Joey reincarnated as a warrior protecting her gold.

"Goldie, I shall call you Goldie." She counted the fingers – ten - and the toes - ten. She peeked at the privates; they were swollen, but the nurse assured her that was normal.

Mother had been silent since those words Joey thought she'd heard her mother mutter at the birth.

"Do you want to hold her?" asked the nurse of Joey's mother.

Her Mother's face was the expression you wear at the top of a roller coaster before the rush of gravity kicked in; it was expectant and frozen, the prepared smile as though nailed in a clown's grin to show her ease, demonstrating the antitheses. All this in a glance, and Joey thought: *She's afraid.*

Joey's mother looked like she wanted to protest, but no words were spoken from the frozen moue. The nurse reset.

"Let's leave her alone with her child," said the perky woman in official clothes.

The mother didn't move, so the woman touched her on her arm, and Joey's mother snailed to the door, dripping relief married to dread, her eyes never leaving Goldie.

Then Joey was alone, with a little life in her arms. Through all the months of pregnancy, she had tried not to imagine this moment, tried not to think of the birth as anything but a relief to discharge the reminder of her violation. Her shame. It was a shameful thing, not what had happened to her, but the result. That was the message sent. That was why they had lied to their friends. That was why Mother tried to have her kill it. That was why they were hiding out in the humidity and slow drawls of South Carolina. Yet here was a baby, an innocent, that was Joey's. Again, she rubbed her cheek against

Goldie, and the child rooted at the touch, the perfect rosebud lips opening.

She wants milk. Then, the realization. *I have milk. She wants my milk.* The decision was conscious. Unashamed of her nakedness, she opened the hospital gown and raised the newborn to her nipple. Goldie clamped on and sucked. She worked hard, and then she drank, and Joey felt joy like she never had. *I'm keeping her. Mother cannot make me give her up.*

After a while, Goldie seemed to lose interest in her breast, but she was still rooting. Joey didn't know what to do. Maybe the other breast had milk? How did it work? She was unprepared. She awkwardly cradled Goldie to her other breast, and again, the newborn suckled contentedly, her clenched fist held against Joey's mouth, the other arm tucked below Joey's other breast. *This is joy. I won't do it wrong. I will not be my mother.*

Then the question: *Had mother ever felt this way about her, Joey?* The door opened, and the apparition of her thoughts materialized, horror on her face.

"Don't feed her."

"I'm keeping her," the words calm, assured.

"Don't bond with her."

"Too late."

"We've discussed this."

"I've changed my mind."

"It's not practical."

"I'm a mother now, mother. She needs me, and I will not fail her."

The words lay between them, the implication clear.

"I will not fail you now," retorted the woman who had failed her in so many ways. "I know what's best."

"You've never known what's best."

"It might seem that way now, but you'll understand when you're…."

"A mother?" offered Joey.

"Joey, Josaphina. I've never claimed to be perfect."

"You haven't?"

"I've made mistakes. But I'm not wrong now. You agreed. We have a family who will take the – the child."

"Goldie. Her name is Goldie."

"We've signed papers. You are not equipped to handle a baby, and I will not take over the duties for you."

"I'll find a way."

"How? You have no education. You have no one to support you and nowhere to live. You don't know how to look after yourself, never mind an infant. What will you do? Live on the street?"

At that precise moment, Goldie broke off her suckling. Joey looked down as Goldie's face turned red, redder than it had been when she first took her into her arms. Her mouth formed a pucker, and then she started to cry.

Joey shushed Goldie and jiggled her, but the cry became a wail.

"It's okay," crooned Joey.

As Goldie continued to wail, Joey looked at her mother, who sat placidly watching her daughter struggle with her child.

Her eyebrows inched up. "Motherhood. Not as easy as it looks."

Joey held the screaming baby at a distance; her arms stretched as though looking at the entire child would make the baby stop crying. Then Joey took her to her chest and rocked her.

"Mother? Please."

Joey's mother gave a tiny shake of her head. "You want to keep her; you look after her."

"I will." Joey jiggled the frantic infant to no avail.

Her mother sat like Mount Rushmore. "I see. You're doing a great job. Motherhood comes naturally to you. It's instinctive."

Joey felt her mother's will, like an iron clamp, grip her heart, and she held her baby tighter, defeat already beginning to take hold of her brain.

The nurse entered, tut-tutting. "Did you feed her?"

Joey nodded.

"Then she needs to be burped. Here, give her to me."

Joey reluctantly handed over Goldie. Efficiently the nurse held Goldie against her chest and with slow, confident strokes rubbed her back. The crying soothed and with a messy white spill, Goldie burped, and peace reigned.

"All it takes is a little know-how," said the nurse with a smile.

"Do you have that know-how?" interjected Joey's mother.

Joey slid desperate eyes to the woman who had given birth to her.

"I'm right, Joey. You're not equipped."

Joey's eyes slid back to Goldie.

"I'm right, Joey."

"Give me my baby," whispered Joey.

The nurse gentled her into Joey's outstretched arms. Joey took the bundle. Her bundle. Her daughter. She crooned softly. Joey was going to lose. It was a simple truth. She looked at her infant that she was about to give away, trying to burn the vision into her brain. She stroked the skin. Kissed the newborn. And then she did it all again. Until finally, hands took her child, and she was empty. She would never be full again.

17

BARE KNUCKLES

NEW YORK: 1986

"I'd never hurt you on purpose."

"How about accidentally?"

"What?"

Joey had emerged from the crowd as Fran approached her apartment. For the past week, Joey had turned up at predictable places, like the grocery store or outside Fran's gym. She just stood there, watching Fran, waiting to be acknowledged. Tonight, Fran figured it was time to talk it out. They were seated calmly in Fran's living room. Neither acknowledged Manhattan looking regal in reflected light.

"I said, 'Would you hurt me accidentally?" repeated Fran.

"It would be an accident."

"But you'd still hurt me?"

"That's not what I meant."

"Thing is, you never mean to, but you do. You hurt people."

"People hurt me."

"Good."

Joey looked like a wounded bird. "What?"

"I said, 'Good.' You deserve to be hurt."

"I don't."

"You sure?"

"Yes."

"I want to hurt you."

"Why?"

"Why not?"

"That's not a reason."

"Sleeping with Michael is a good reason."

"I did it for you. I know him. He couldn't be faithful. If I hurt you, I'm sorry. It's nothing compared with what he would do. Look at you now. Before children, before you grow old."

"He might not have hurt me. Maybe I wouldn't care. Maybe I would live with it."

Joey had never thought of that option. Fran was good and pure. She would never live with a cheater.

"You couldn't, you're too good. You're the only one who ever saw me as I am."

"The woman who gave her child away?"

"What?"

"Some guy came here bleating about how worried he was about you. How you never turned up for some shoot, and he was counting on you to be there."

"Christian? I don't understand. Why—?"

"Whatever," Fran interrupted her. "I told him not to worry. I said you could not be counted on to do the right thing, only the selfish thing – every time. Every fucking time. I told him he was lucky you disappointed him early because that was all you were capable of. You are like a tidal wave of disappointment, and then I fucked him because I could, and who knows? He may have fucked me someday, and someplace in the future, he may have hurt you." Fran's anger fed on itself, making her immune to the woman crumbling in front of her. "Don't look so hurt."

"Don't hurt me, Fran."

"It's for your own good. If I don't, someone else will, so I'm doing it now – because I love you," she said it insincerely, mirroring Joey's logic.

Joey started to cry.

"Don't you fucking cry. Stop it," yelled Fran.

"I'm sorry. I said so already."

"It's not good enough."

"Why are you mad at me and not Michael?"

"I didn't expect anything from him. Fidelity – yeah, but there's all kinds of betrayal, Joey. There's the kind where you lead people to places they might never go. Charlie in Hamburg, for instance."

"You misread her - just like you misread Mike. She took no convincing. If it hadn't been me, it would have been someone else or something else. She was looking to get burnt, looking to get corrupted."

"And I guess Mike was too?"

Joey examined Fran and her fury. Joey made a decision. The tears dried up. Her voice grew firm. "Want to talk truth, Fran? Let's talk about you."

"Me?"

"Yes. Did I lead where you would never have gone, or did you let me believe that I was the leader? And when Charlie arrived, were you mad because I did what you were planning on doing all the time? Be who you are, Fran. Face some realities. Mike betrayed you. You were going to marry him. The truth, Fran. Are you mad at me because you care more about me than him? Maybe me fucking Mike made you remember what it was like to fuck me?"

"No, Joey. You fucking Mike reminded me of what a fuck-up you are. Where are your friends? Where are your lovers, your family? Best of all, where's your kid? Oh, that's right, you gave it away. It wasn't convenient."

"It wasn't like that."

"It never is with you, Joey. If you ask me, you did the right thing. It may be the one good thing you've done cause God knows you'd make a lousy mother – whoring around to make a point that only you can see. That kid should be down on its knees thanking God that his mother kicked him out, 'cause you suck at everything, Joey, and the only way a kid of yours would have a chance, is if he had nothing to do with you – ever."

The silence was filled with Fran's furious breathing.

"Her. The baby was a girl. Her name is Goldie."

"What a crap name."

Joey reacted as though she were shot. Her mouth opened in a silent cry that echoed across her face, then ate inward through her eyes. Fran knew she'd done what she set out to do. She'd achieved revenge. She'd finally hurt Joey. Joey clutched her stomach and looked around blindly, then she turned and stumbled from the apartment.

Fran watched her go. Revenge: fleeting pleasure; dire consequences – tempered by eons of regret.

She sat alone. Fran knew the stages. When she shot her father, the blood spilling across the floor, him groaning half-conscious, regret already congealing, pain solidifying, and finally, an understanding of the courage that it took to inflict hurt. 'Deny. Deny. Deny.' Her father had taught her the concept. It was not only a recipe for nullifying culpability against the pain inflicted on others, but it was also the mantra for dealing with the anguish that came after the free-basting, the high, the release, of inflicting violence on another. Verbally or physically.

18

THE REASON

Joey stumbled from Fran's apartment. She'd been wrong. Each time she thought she saw the way, understood the solution, she'd been wrong. A cab stopped in front of her, and the passenger exited. Joey was crying again. She crept into the yellow taxi and gave her address, then settled back, trying to understand why her logic always made her do the wrong thing when, in her mind, it seemed like the right thing. She tried to identify when the pattern began as the cab sailed the potholes of Manhattan.

Paths traveled, bridges not crossed. Confident on all the wrong things, that she and Giovanni would be good together. That Mother would not have helped her had she chosen to keep her daughter.

That when she saw Michael kiss a girl through the window of a cab, she should have looked away.

And....

That she shouldn't have believed that she could prevent the future pain Michael would inflict on Fran.

Joey flashed back to the moment she'd decided that if Mike made a move, she'd let him.

It was Joey's first week back in New York after The House of Rest. Joey was in a cab on her way to the MET on 5th Avenue. She could've walked. It would've helped her get rid of those stubborn last pounds, but no medication, no booze, no drugs meant life had to be lived as it was. Walking in New York free of drugs took effort. The crowd's bustle-bombardment was too much on her senses. The cab slammed on breaks, and Joey grabbed onto the passenger strap to steady herself, her face almost hitting the side window with the force of the sudden stop. She tensed on the back seat as she braced herself against the passenger door. In front of her was a man who looked like Mike, but couldn't be him, because he was kissing a girl - *not* Fran.

After that very successful reunion with Fran, where Mike had remained watchful and indulgent in her presence, Joey had concluded that maybe she'd imagined his expression in the halo of the lighter when he'd looked at her like she was a Kobe steak. Once Fran had joined them, his hooded eyes had avoided Joey's. She was glad to be wrong about him. Maybe Mike had changed? Or. Could it be that he had avoided her gaze because she read him so well?

Before, when she and Mike could make a club desirable simply by frequenting it, Mike and Joey had communicated with laughter-filled glances across a crowd, a naughty team, wreaking havoc, just for fun. He'd catch her eye and Joey'd cross a room and whisper in his ear, tongue him as some newbie who'd believed she'd found her one-true-love, realized her time was up. Mike would return the favor. Their glances spoke volumes - like the Bat signal - they could read each other from a distance. When she needed escape, he'd slip up behind her, grab her across the torso or cup her ass. She would laugh as some guy she'd grown bored of would try and figure out the appropriate response. The instinct was to defend her, but she wasn't pushing Mike away. She'd let her eyes stay on the guy while Mike created a picture of what the stranger had thought he'd do to Joey himself. "Don't be mad," she'd pout at the stranger. Then she and Mike would leave, racing along to some new place. People would pour in, music blasted, and the night would run out in a haze. It was all a blur until they left in a silver moonscape sky, to heave and sleep and leave and never say goodbye.

Joey *knew* Mike.

So when the cab jerked away, she stopped it and walked back to verify it was indeed Mike wrapped around a girl, maybe 17, who would soon be the new face on covers and billboards. Her path to that end begun in the embrace of Mike's arms. Mike and the model walked down 5th Avenue, long and linked. Joey wondered how she could tell Fran. She had no proof. It was not like she had a camera to document their sticky moments at traffic lights, smooching through the 'walk' sign twice.

She had not misread Mike. He had not changed.

A plan hatched at that moment, watching her friend's fiancé feeling up a teenager as New Yorkers hustled past them. Joey recalled the cycle of look-alike blondes that had appeared and disappeared during the final months with Giovanni. She knew what it was like to have to pretend that you didn't notice what everyone saw. She wouldn't let Fran walk the path that had taken Joey to the House of Rest.

Right there on the sidewalk in Manhattan, she began to plan. She was sure it would work. Maybe she didn't need to *tell* Fran. Maybe she needed to *show* her. *Don't shoot the messenger* sprang to mind. Yeah. If she told Fran, her friend wouldn't believe her. It would sour what looked to be the beginning of good - and good with Fran was better than great with most.

Maybe she, Joey, could be the hero? Maybe Fran would turn to *her*, and the moments promised in Hamburg could become forever. With Fran, Joey would be complete and never have to visit The House of Rest again.

Joey had to be creative. She had to *show* Fran who Mike really was, and then Joey could be Fran's forever after. But she had to be smart and show Fran who Mike really was, without getting caught in the crosshairs herself. An idea brewed. She wouldn't encourage Mike at all, but if he came at her, she'd find a way for Fran to discover that Mike was not who he portrayed himself to be. Better for Fran to discover that truth before Fran needed to lie to herself about who her husband really was.

***

That had been Joey's plan. Help Fran. Even if it meant fucking Michael. Joey pulled her Madonna look-alike shoulder-emphasized coat tightly around her as though the fabric could shield her. The sex didn't mean anything. It was a mercy fuck. For Fran. Instead, everything had gone wrong. Again. Joey couldn't believe the things Fran had said to her. As the cab slammed on breaks, Joey felt that old familiar 'disconnect' take hold. She had tried to do something good for Fran and it had come out wrong. She'd tried to tell Christian the truth of who she was - and all he saw was the image. She'd said 'No' on the rooftop. She had. She knew she had.

Escape!

She needed to escape, but where? How?

The cab stopped outside her apartment. She didn't want to go to the emptiness that awaited her. She wanted to blur life and feelings. Joey needed to feel numb.

19

FRAN, ALLY & CHRISTIAN

Fran's freckles were magnified and multiplied. Her hair coiffed like coils of sunshine around her head. She modeled finely woven fabric by the best in haute couture for an editorial spread for Haute Vie. Her lips and nails were painted black. Her eyes feathered dirty green, dripping down her cheeks in artful smudges. They teamed the precious designer dream creations with torn fishnet stockings and men's work boots, laces undone, the tongues arching out like a tongue in search of water.

The setting was skid row. The homeless slunk furtively, yelling at no one and everyone, while the addicts' comatose haze saw nothing. The juxtaposition of plenty and little, creating magic in the lens.

"Look left; raise your hand to your eyes." Fran looked left. An addict stood out in the backdrop. The elegance of the body amongst society's throw-away people, noticeable. Fran focused, mildly curious at the object d'art that her mind's eye recognized. Dirty blonde hair – matted; long fingers - grubby. Fran watched as the hands tied a belt around a long arm - a needle inserted.

"Look right," called the photographer, but Fran couldn't.

The addict lolled her head back, the perfect filtered light bounced off the walls as the sun crept out from the clouds and created an echo of The Pieta - with the addict as Christ but with Mary absent. The grubby beauty was highlighted as though sharing the very same shoot that Fran was in; then the sun slipped back behind the clouds and the alley was thrown into shadow.

“Fran? Turn your head to the right.”

Fran pulled her suction cup gaze away from the blackness of the ally and turned to the lens, ice dripping through her veins, clamming up her brain. *Was that Joey?*

“Sexy,” Instructed the photographer.

She arched and lifted the skirt of her dress to show a stocking-ripped thigh, hand on her hip, mouth garish in a standard sexual snarl.

“Oh baby, beautiful. Yes! Yes! Oh, gorgeous.”

The camera clicked, and Fran’s magnet eyes were drawn back to where the addict lay. She squinted, trying to penetrate the shadows to ascertain if the woman was indeed Joey, while her brain went to war with itself.

Not my problem. Fran counseled herself. *Look away. Avoid the image*. Fran conjured her fury at Joey’s betrayal as a reminder that she had cut Joey from her life. For good this time. Forever. No matter what. She deliberately turned her head away.

But now the photographer insisted that she stared in the direction of Joey. “Profile, baby. No. The other way. Yes! Chin up. Haughty. Haughty. There. Hold. Hold. Beautiful.”

Fran’s mouth was a beach – dry and grainy. Each time she looked away, all she saw was Joey. It’s what she saw when the shoot was over, what she saw when she tossed her model bag on the hardwood floor of her apartment.

In the reflected halo of the sky that’s never dark from New York City lights, Fran packed away her boots and pulled on her Chinese slippers. She stripped naked and pressed up against the cold glass that kept out the world with its constant noise. Trying to push at the windowpane as if capturing an elusive idea – a memory from Europe that she had played over and rejected, retrieved and buried. Dog-worn images dragged out and categorized as: ‘No Can Do.’ They whirled around in Fran’s head; the hub: Joey. She tried to masturbate against the cold glass, her hand moving, playing, trying – nothing. No one appeared in the windows to watch. No one to witness the woman trying to obliterate what her mind had seen. Would release expunge the guilt of what she had done?

She felt frosted by her effort to deny the effect of Joey, or maybe it was just that she was still naked leaning against a window in the Manhattan sky. Fran pulled the throw from the couch and covered herself, giving in to the memories. Joey and Fran, Fran and Joey. Yin and yang in Hamburg. Together. Allies. Friends. And more.

Fran awakened on the couch, her neck at an awkward angle. Had it been real? So much of the time spent with Joey seemed to have taken place in the non-world. Of sighs and release and never-happened's. Of fresh days and internal denial. Deny, deny, deny like it had never been. Had she dreamed Joey in the alley shooting up, or lived it? Her eyes moved to the smudge of clouds against a dirty, egg-yolk sky. The buildings, with their early morning lights, drew the gaze to the illuminating sparkle of apartments as citizens began their day. Her gaze lingered above the refuse that was the reality; that was the city.

Fran pushed the cushion, so she was comfortable and watched the battle for light and dark play out in the distance. Though dawn had broken, the light stayed in mourning, and the heavens cried in rain. She shivered naked beneath the throw she had stolen from Joey all those years ago in Hamburg.

Since their fight, fanned by her fury, Fran had looked for Joey. Not consciously. But actually? Yes, consciously. After Fran had made the forced phone apology, she'd ghosted Joey. Yet Joey had stalked her, turning up at all of Fran's haunts in an effort to speak to her after the train wreck of Mike. Joey would stand there, not moving, waiting to be acknowledged. Fran would walk by so close to her that it might seem like Fran would stop, but she kept right on going, her gaze never acknowledging Joey's presence. As the days eked by, Fran had grown accustomed to the long silhouette of Joey lurking. She'd taken pleasure in ignoring her.

But after their argument, Joey had suddenly disappeared. That surprised Fran. Whenever they'd fought in Hamburg and Fran had withdrawn, Joey would follow a pattern. She'd slink around Fran's periphery, waiting to be petted and brought back into the fold. Not this time. Weeks had passed.

If Fran was honest, she was afraid of what she'd done. Her rage had been like her actions with her father. Vengeful. Corrosive. Intentional. She might not have shot Joey, but the effect had been the same. She had intended to wound her, and Fran knew her words had found their mark. Her fury was like a flame to gasoline. Explosive. Dangerous. Destructive. Once assuaged, it could not be undone. That's why Fran hung onto control so tightly. Fran, out of control, blazed violently, and when her feeling had been satiated, like Humpty-Dumpty after the fall, you couldn't put things back as they'd been before.

She was afraid to face Joey again after what she'd said, but secretly, she'd waited for Joey to appear, as she always had. When she didn't, Fran's guilt projected Joey onto strangers on the street, so she'd pause to acknowledge Joey, only to concede that it was just her mind playing tricks, making her see what she wanted to see, that she might never see again.

Could the woman in the alley be Joey? She considered the blueprint of their relationship. Fran had seen Joey plunge from the highs in a second, and her lows could get extreme. When Fran had read about the demise of Joey's marriage to Giovanni, the spectacle of it, she recognized the trait that had been fomented in their days in Hamburg. Fran had played interceptor back then, interrupting the psychological and emotional fall before it became too extreme. From what she knew of Joey, it was quite possible that the reason Joey was not lingering in Fran's periphery, trying to patch the breech, was because Joey had gone on a binge. Not that Joey would be homeless, but she was capable of getting lost in a loop of 'high' that could take her anywhere.

Even to an alley on a skid row?

Fran had to admit that if Joey had bottomed out, Fran was partially responsible. She rubbed the soft blanket across her cheek -

any remnants of anger disintegrated as she recalled the two of them touching beneath this very cover.

After coming, she lay for a second, panting. When she stood, she was Fran again. Practical. In control. She would go and get Joey. Rescue seemed too strong a word, and although she had always played the protector in their duo, the recent escapade with Michael made her acknowledge that it was possible that it had always been Joey pulling the strings. Fran wanted to be the protector. Joey wanted to be coddled. Each had played their role.

As Fran pulled on her Calvin jeans, a fitted cashmere sweater with shoulder emphases, and Princess Di flats, she admitted that Joey affected her in ways that made the latter scared. There was no way Fran could abandon Joey in a needle-infested alley – though that's exactly what she'd done yesterday. Today was new. She recalled one of her life-affirming mantras:

Do not let yesterday's mistakes hold you back from today's adventures.
Failure is just another way to learn.

The smart thing was not to interact with Joey, but she acknowledged that Joey *had* acted to protect her, just as she had shot her father to protect her mother. Fran's fury had dissipated during the night, leaving only concern.

Joey and Fran. Fran and Joey. Their relationship, as sporadic as it was, spanned a decade, and when it was good - it was the best. The same things that made Fran vulnerable to artistic men made her appreciate Joey. Fran was plenty practical. Anyone hanging onto neatness and control like she did, desperately trying to create order from the messiness of life, had to be practical. And yet she had always opened the door to uncontrolled Joey. Maybe it was as complex as trying to recreate the chaos of her childhood. She found it hard to submit control, even during sex. Joey was the only one who could always make her lose control and had drowned her in pleasure. That was enough of a reason not to leave her in the alleyway. Maybe it was time to explore the truth of Joey.

The alley in the greasy ink of early light was like a movie set, but for the acrid urine that scorched the nostrils and the needles littering the ground, waiting to spread their disease. Fran picked her way through the human debris and called softly, "Joey? Joey?"

I never loved Michael the way I should. I liked the way he looked, the compliments he gave - his softness. His status. There was talk of him moving to directing. The cachet and image to create the respectability I'd always craved. The safety and security of normal I need to present to the world when I launch my line. I knew he would never hurt me in a way that left a mark.

When Mike left, it was Joey who occupied her dreams, not her former fiancé.

I'd been away from home for almost two years trying to find my way to design when Joey arrived at the Pension Haben in Hamburg. Most girls arrived a little scared, but Joey strutted in wearing a mini so short it almost didn't exist and a gauzy flowing top that scooped away from the body, so you caught upturned breasts unexpectedly. She teamed the look with flat Mary Janes. She had a cloth bag slung over her shoulder. She smiled fresh as though she believed in something. Joey walked over to the communal board covered with the Polaroids from the shoots the models had done, and without asking, she'd pinned a paper over our photos. I would've complained, but when I moved to confront her, my eye was drawn to the art. It was a Munch reversal of his period documenting his troubled relationship with Tulla Larsen. The work was reminiscent of 'Salome-Paraphrase,' or 'The Vampire,' even 'Separation,' with the theme of hair trapping, entwining, and ultimately binding. Joey took the concept further. Hers had a man finely drawn on an iron bed with a giant erection, ejaculating sperm like Munch's hair, imprisoning, omnipotent, almost evil, so the ejaculation oozed around the room in growing arcs to a woman in profile, where it gagged her, penetrated and bound her, ripping her brutally apart. It was disturbing, and like Munch's 'The Scream,' you could not look away.

"What's it called?" asked the Swede who had joined us at the board.

"Man," I said.

Joey turned and looked at me, and we recognized each other.

In the alley, Fran came upon the woman from yesterday, the long limbs – grubby like a chimney sweep, the blonde hair in tight, soiled coils, spread like the spokes of an opened umbrella, ratted. Fran did not go nearer, too moved to speak. Guilt blocked Joey's name in her throat. She could not ignore her part in this. Joey had slept with Michael, and Fran's fuse had suddenly and terribly flamed. Her intensity had been more targeted on Joey, for their unspoken time in Hamburg made them wary allies. Somehow, she expected men to betray her, but friends were held to a higher standard. So, she had unleashed on Joey. Joey wasn't like other people. She couldn't shake it off.

Fran had to admit that part of her fury was discovering that Joey had kept a secret from her yet told a man, Christian, that Joey, of all people, was, in fact, a mother. When the tall, black man in beautiful clothes with a voice like warm embers had announced that fact, as though Fran would know, resentment had fomented inside her. No matter what she pretended, she believed that she and Joey were intimates. Had she told Joey about her past? No. But she thought she knew everything that there was to know about the woman who made her loins liquid. To whom she'd played protector. Yet, Joey was a mother. And she'd never shared that secret with Fran. Emotion spewed up. Love and hate fused as she looked at Joey lying amongst the debris in the dank alley. What else did she not know about this woman that she had allowed herself to love?

Fran tried to speak, but words did not form. She cleared her throat and stepped forward. "Joey?" Nothing. The matted hair covered the face. Now that Fran was in front of Joey, she hesitated. Just as her act of violence so long ago had altered her life forever, Fran's suppressed fury had once again spilled over, finally pushing Joey down the path she was always destined to walk. The inevitability of it was no comfort.

"Joey," she said it softly, like waking a slumbering child.

It was not enough to rouse Joey from whatever stupor she was in. Fran forced herself forward. She reached a hand onto the foul-smelling garments and gently shook Joey. A groan rumbled from the blonde tangles like a bear battling hibernation. Then the body went slack.

"Joey!" Fran shook her roughly. "Wake up. It's me, Fran."

She reached over and pulled the matted hair from Joey's face, and finally, the blonde opened somnolent eyes. They were shocking. Brown instead of the sea turquoise she'd expected. This was not Joey. The woman muttered something unintelligible and grasped Fran's wrist with surprising strength.

Fear and repulsion washed over Fran. Relief too. Joey was most likely living it up somewhere. She was foolish to think that the ultimate manipulator would crash so quickly. This woman had been living on the street for a while. Joey hadn't disappeared that long ago. She could be anywhere. But even Joey left word with someone. Her booker. Someone. But no one had heard from her in a while. Fran looked into the bleary eyes. Guilt having brought her here, guilt refusing to let her leave.

"Let me help you. Come with me."

Whatever was addling the blonde's brain, Fran's words were not penetrating. She was not reading Fran as a savior. She was reading Fran as a violator.

"Get off me!" The woman lunged at Fran with a skinny arm and connected just below Fran's jaw.

The pain was blinding. Fran winced as a string of expletives hit her on foul breath, the grip, an unexpected vice. Fran leaned into the woman and then jerked in the opposite direction, breaking the contact. Fran turned and stumbled from the alley.

20

SOLUTIONS

"I'm hiring a detective." Christian was ugly and beautiful with an air that time could fragment in front of him and life would still be bent to his will. It wasn't a power that was intimidating. It was reassuring. He was still; no restless movement at all.

"Your mind seems made up. Why are you telling me?"

"You're her friend. She loves you."

Fran felt the pressure push down like glass on dough. "And?"

His crooked teeth flashed, though not in a smile. "You're cold."

Fran felt the anger spark like a flame receiving a gentle breeze when you thought the fuel had burnt out. "What do you know of anything? Who are you to judge?"

"Someone has to. Someone has to say: enough. Stop. This is not right."

He was dressed in an elegant denim shirt, buttoned to the collar - likely Ralph Lauren - which he'd paired with a deep red jacket, the color of a healed wound. Black trousers and matching suede loafers completed the look. The colors contrasting against his black skin made the clash of hues harmonious. Unconsciously sensual. She reminded herself that he had come to his power position as a result of fashion. His personal taste immaculate, while still giving a nod to the company's founding line: Boot Shoot. He stood there so confident that he knew what was best. She could feel her anger rise.

"Look in the mirror. You're the one hiring the models. Pick a girl that isn't heroine-thin. Stop creating some image no one can fulfill. Stop butting in when no one asked you to and change something that matters."

"Joey matters."

"I still don't get it. You hardly know her – why do you care?"

"No one else seems to. I thought maybe you did. I think you do."

She had agreed to see him again out of guilt coupled with the idea that maybe he could shed some light on where Joey was. Fran would walk down a street and still think she saw Joey – but it was always some long-legged blonde – not Joey. It was like some flying saucer had sucked her up, and she was gone. Part of Fran delighted in the idea of Joey in a figure-hugging silver suit, finally at peace with some alien herd.

"I think we should find her kid."

"What?"

He didn't repeat himself. "I need something to go on. I've got her social security number—"

"How did you get that?"

"She worked for my company, remember? But I'm not sure that's enough. I figured you would know something that might help?"

Fran shook her head. "Christian, you're crossing lines. You had no right to track me down, and you have no right to try and find her kid."

"I disagree. Joey's got this image as if she has her act together—"

"She doesn't. That's not the image that anyone who knows her has of Joey," she interrupted him with just the slightest basting of sarcasm.

"Exactly. That's the point. It's like she has child-logic. Like no one ever taught her how the world functions. Once I knew your name, it didn't take a genius to figure you were the model, Fran Childres. I had my guy track you down. I've put him on Joey."

"Did she ask for your help?"

"She didn't have to. You don't tell a stranger you gave away your child unless you've made some decisions about finding the kid. Why she hasn't before is anyone's guess, but logic says that's next on her list. She doesn't seem to have anyone looking out for her."

Fran's mouth got small in what was supposed to project as an ironic smile. "So you are going to? Out of the goodness of your heart?"

He shook his head. "You people. Callous. I'm in a position to change things when I can. It's what our company does. We see areas of exploitation and we go in and try and ameliorate the consequences. One of our subsidiaries is devoted to philanthropy. It's not common knowledge. Boot Shoot is just one of many companies under the international conglomerate that we've built. Joey's.... She's not what she seems. She - she touched me. And before you suggest it, I'm not talking about her outsides. I think I can help. I'm going to try. I'm talking to some of the people she started out with – some of her clients, someone called Roma, and, of course, Mike." He waited for a reaction and when none came, he continued. "She seemed closest to you."

"She wasn't."

"She said you were the one good person she knew. The one who never wanted anything from her, who gave unconditionally."

"She sure knew how to take." The bitterness spawned by the truth of the words slithered from her mouth.

"Yeah. I imagine she's good at that. But I figure you enjoyed being taken from."

"Which means what?"

"There's a reason she thought like she did about you. Some part of you encouraged it. She speaks about you in unreal terms. No one is that perfect. You got something from having her around. If she was such a mess, someone like you wouldn't let her in."

"You breeze into her life, and suddenly you're the expert?"

"I identify. People see what they want to see. My parents - they talk with an accent; it makes them a target. Me – I'm moving in hallowed circles. Do you know how many times I've turned up for a meeting and they address an assistant because he's white and they don't expect a billionaire to look like me? I've been given the keys to park people's cars when I'm standing at the valet waiting for my own. I know what it's like not to be seen. If you listen to her, she asks the questions no one else asks. She sees things others don't think to notice and not the obvious things. I spent a very short time with her. I recognized her insides. She should have everything, but she had nothing. No self-esteem. Just pain hiding behind a bad-ass attitude. The way she spoke about you makes me think you saw in her what I saw. Giving your kid up – I don't know how that happened, but that could corrupt someone."

"We all have pain."

"She couldn't handle hers."

"So you're going to rescue her?" She shook her head ironically. "Someone always wants to rescue Joey. And someone always gets hurt - usually, it's not Joey."

He didn't waste time with further debate. "Will you help me? Anything. A relative?"

"Her mother lives in Connecticut. But Joey hates her."

"Why?"

"Never said."

"Think her mother knew she was pregnant?"

"When would it be? Her pregnancy? Must've been before Hamburg. Before '75? '76?"

Christian did the math in his head. "That would make her what? Thirteen - fourteen? Her mother would have to know."

"Then that's where you should start."

21

THE HOUSE OF REST REVISITED

Joey was painting symbolism, not abstract. A velvet rabbit astride a giant blade. The rabbit, surrounded by women of wealth, their status visible from their nonchalant poses, their pearls, and their elaborate costumes. Their hands clasped firmly to a bottle or glass; their heads turned away with one horrified eye on the scene with the rabbit. Half a mouth in a moue of angst while the other half, the far side of the face, the public side, smiled impenetrably. The knife held by an arm that led to the shadows. A man, verdite on black, lurked, his eye on the impaled rabbit. He gripped the knife by the hilt, the free hand arched out of the darkness, and grasped the nipple of the dominant society queen. His arm the only part of him in the light, picking at the dowager's puckered nipple – her breast sagging and flaccid, exposed, amongst the clothed chorus of look-alike-ladies.

It was while Joey was caught in the art she had abandoned in Europe and now sought refuge in, that the new nurse, with bright irises of a Halloween creature, came and whispered, "You have a guest."

Joey ripped herself from the work she was vomiting onto the canvas. She had the 'Alice' feel of being so far down the rabbit hole that she'd disappeared. She resurfaced, like Houdini slipping free from handcuffs – yet his trick had ultimately killed him, and Joey was trying very hard not to seek death.

Before she said the word, she knew she was wrong. "Fran?"

"Christian. He says he's a friend."

Didn't he know how things worked? She'd rejected him. Normal response? Move on. It's the right thing to do. Common sense? Right? It's what Fran had done. It's what everyone has ever done. Not crooked-teeth-guy. She'd fucked him over, hadn't she? Yet he just kept coming back.

Joey applied highlights to the hand controlling the knife. She'd replicated Michael Angelo's Sistine Chapel hand. Then she added ecstasy to the face of the social matron and to the side of the face of the lurking man, letching at the rabbit. It was intricate work, subtly obvious, though she would never have the courage to call it Mother and her Man.

The rabbit's me.

The nurse wondered if Joey heard her. "Christian would like to see you. Will you see him?"

"No."

The nonperson turned for the door, her round thighs rubbing against each other in a swish-swish sound, and then she stopped. "He told me if you said 'no,' that he had news of Fran."

"Fran?"

The young girl knew she was not supposed to coax, but she had been at The House of Rest for two months, and Joey was the only patient without visitors. What did she know? She was a 'go-for' on the ladder of power, but she recognized Joey. She'd had pictures of Joey on her wall for years. She dreamt that if her stout thighs were as lean and long as the supermodel's, her life would be perfect. She cut her hair in the layers Joey wore. She colored her hair the exact same shade. She even saved up and bought a knock-off of the clothing Joey wore in the picture on her wall. Her fantasy that she was a version of Joey made life easier. Now, here she was two months into her transfer, hoping that the well-dressed man in expensive clothes might be the key to transforming the supermodel back into the perfect image on her wall. 'Cause what did it say about her if she had chosen someone to dream about whose life was so bad that she hid away in The House of Rest? If the supermodel sucked and she was what the candy striper aspired toward, then there was no chance that life would ever be other than what it was for her at that moment, and that thought was unacceptable.

Joey concentrated on the Madam's face, highlighting the façade garishly, then working on the rolling eye fastened in horror on the rabbit, like the horse in Delacroix's *Arab Horses Fighting in a Stable* that she'd seen at the Musée d'Orsay.

"He seems nice," said the nurse of Christian.

"He is."

"He said he had news of Fran," she repeated. "Is that Fran Childres, the model?"

Joey stood back from the canvas. *Art imitating life*. That would be the title. The painting was done. She looked at the girl hovering in the doorway. She made a decision. "I'll see him."

Joey entered the yellow room, unsure of herself. The Boot Shoot seemed so long ago. Christian had been that rare male. He'd listened to her, and she'd felt heard. She could not recall if she'd disappointed him in some consequential way. She didn't think so, just in the usual way.

The tall man next to the Ficus tree looked like he was color-coded to match the surroundings. He was dressed in a crisp white shirt, cashmere jacket and Chinos. Sockless brown loafers in butter leather completed the Polaroid. His clothing palette reminiscent of Richard Roundtree in *Shaft in Africa*. She felt humor bubble in her depths. Maybe hysteria.

The visitor's room was the only room with color, she noted. He reached for her hand, and when she ignored the gesture, he bear-hugged her in a smother that evoked child-like longing. She did not reciprocate, rather waited until he pulled back to look at her with the word, "Joey."

She sat.

He mimicked her, lowering himself onto the plush wingback. He steepled his fingers, then created fists, and finally placed his palms, fingers splayed, on his thighs.

"How are you?"

"How did you find me?

"I – you didn't turn up for the shoot."

"I canceled the booking." She'd made the effort. "I'm sorry."

The silence stretched. He's not good at small talk.

"I met your mother." He said it like she should be excited.

Joey's ocean eyes crested the wave to his gaze. She took her time reaching his eyes as a million contradictory thoughts ricocheted, fighting each other to be stated simultaneously.

You're supposed to be on my side. Understand me. And this is your opening gambit?

She settled on, "How did that happen?"

"Fran suggested—" He raised his hands like a priest about to deliver a sermon, some story she was sure she didn't want to hear.

"You saw Fran?"

"Don't you want to know about your mother?"

"No."

"About your daughter?"

Joey felt the guillotine-slash-cut. The entitlement of this man.

"I think your mother knows."

"Think? You came here with 'think'? What do you know about Goldie?"

"Goldie? Ahh, your daughter? Nothing – yet. I believe your mother knows, but she's not willing to say."

Joey looked away. This was all shades of wrong. This was crossing lines and personal infringement, and he seemed unaware, as though he had a right. "Christian, why are you here?"

"To help."

"Why?"

"To get you out."

"Why?"

"I care."

"You can't rescue me."

"I can try."

"Fuck!" She hit her hand down on the table next to her, so the vase, with its happy daisies, jumped. "Don't help. I didn't ask for help. Do you think I haven't figured out that my mother knows what happened to my child? I'm not dumb. Why does everyone think I'm stupid? I'm not here because I'm stupid. I'm here 'cause I'm not mother material."

"How do you know?"

"I know."

"You could be wrong."

"I could be right."

"I don't think you are."

"And as a man, you *know*, right?"

"Joey, my gender has nothing to do with it. Give yourself a chance." He crossed to her.

"I'm doing better than that. I'm giving my daughter a chance. I can't take care of myself; look where I am. I'm no role model. I'm not what I want in a mother."

"You're great."

She laughed. "What part of me is great? The lying-cheating-drug-taking part, or the part you want to fuck?"

"The part that smiles out in the photographs."

"Oh, the image."

"No. It's the same part that tried to protect your friend. I see what you are to the world, but I see more. I see how you are inside. Your daughter would, too."

"I'm sure she would. She could come here and stay with me in The House of Rest. 'Look, Goldie, it's mummy. She can't make it in the real world. Aren't you glad I found you? Don't you want to be a fuck-up like me?'"

"We could wait 'til you're healthy."

"What do you think I've been waiting for? Every day, I start out thinking that this is the day I'll do it right. And the fear of seeing her and not being enough. I'd rather have the dream of a future than the certainty of rejection."

"It may not happen – the rejection."

"Look at me, Christian. Am I what you look for in a mother?"

"You could be."

"Could, should, would. Is, am, me. Someday, I'll be okay, and I'll know it. I'll find Goldie. Right now, I just can't seem to get to someday."

"You can make it happen. It's up to you."

"But no pressure, right?"

"It's kind of simple, Joey. If you want your daughter, you have to fight for her." Christian took a beat. "You fight for her like you fought for Fran."

"That was real successful. That worked out." She looked at him. "How's Fran?"

"You haven't been reading the papers?"

"Not exactly."

"Fran left New York. She got her collection together. There's a lot of buzz."

"Fran was a long way from finding an investor." He was studying his hand like it was a great piece of sculpture. Joey's laugh was like the air being popped. "Does she know you're bankrolling it? Do you think she would take your money if she knew where it was coming from?"

"She knows. Not everyone is willing to postpone a dream."

"It's not about her dream or her design; it's about control. Yours."

"It's about her talent. Boot Shoot manufactures all our clothing in the south-west. We've been thinking of going in a different direction for a while, expanding for the mass market. Her designs, our marketing. It could be huge."

Joey spoke slowly, a theory proffered, "You think if Fran is not in New York, I'll get better. I'll be manageable?"

"Maybe."

"Last time I was in here, it wasn't about Fran."

"This time it is."

"No. I'm – when I was here I – I discovered something. I didn't know it at the time, but I got a map while I was here, a go-to set of rules I can apply when things get crazy. Questions to ask that I never thought to ask before. Some events happened since I left The House of Rest, that -. Well, before I'd just bury them and think it was me. That I deserved to be punished. But it's not about punishment. My stay here last time helped me see that. I think – I'm trying to fix what's not right. I'm not there yet. I'm not going to contaminate my child. I'm not going to mess up her life. Neglect, abuse, whatever made me this way, and my mother before me, this cycle is stopping with me. Hopefully, Goldie, wherever she is, is healthy - physically, and psychologically. I can't believe we're like some rotten seed - born this way. Made this way. I remember a time when I saw the world as good. When I was good."

"Who said you were bad? You made some choices hundreds of people make every day. They don't beat themselves up. I don't think you've got something that needs to be fixed – have you looked around – you've not chosen the most moral or stable of professions. No one else is locking themselves up, not even the ones that should be. Especially them."

"Why are you here? I didn't ask for your help." Weariness sculpted her words, sagging her shoulders. She raised a useless hand. "Get the fuck out of here. Ok? What I do or don't do has NOTHING to do with you. Back off."

"Through our philanthropy, I've seen hundreds of women do what you do and not cut themselves up about it. The fact that you're here shows there is nothing wrong with you. I've got the feeling that no one has been on your side. You've been told all the things that are wrong with you, and I think you should be told that you're not so different from everyone else."

"Thank you."

"You know what I mean. People – more than you know – have given up their kids for adoption."

"I never had a choice!" The fierce correction.

“So go get her. Get out of here and go introduce yourself. I’ve heard all your excuses and it comes down to one thing. Fear. I’m going to hang around here until you see what I see.”

“You know what I see – just another man trying to fit me into his mold.”

“That’s not true. There’s only one way to prove I’m not what you say. I’m going to be here every day until you have the courage to go after what you want directly. Not in some backhanded way, but upfront. I want you to know there is someone who believes in you.” He stood up. “I’ll see you tomorrow.”

Joey almost expected the swell of an orchestra to fill the air. Like in a movie. Was this guy for real? He said that he heard her, but he didn’t listen. She *needed* to be in The House of Rest, as a refuge, yet he had sought her out. Insisted that he would not leave her alone. How dare he?

She kept her eyes down and he took it for compliance or some deep emotion she was not anywhere close to feeling. “I’ll be back every day to remind you who you are, rather than what the world has made you think you are.” When she finally spoke, she’d composed her face into a ‘covergirl’ brightness that he mislabeled as hope.

“Christian?”

“Yeah.” His lips parted in a Clint Eastwood clench.

“I never imagined someone would come and say what you’ve said, promise what you’ve promised,” she said it with a huge dose of sincerity, like the punch line in a commercial: I’d given up on ever getting streak free glasses - until I discovered GLEAM! She added Marilyn Monroe eyes, opened a little too wide to convey guileless candor. She reached over and laid a hand on his forearm. “I want you to do something for me.”

He sat back down. “Anything.”

Her eyes were the color of the ocean when you put it in a bottle and took it home from the beach. Her expression was one of warmth and lazy afternoons, of being known and of heat, and Christian knew he had reached her. Whatever she asked for, he would give her. He needed to make her believe that he was different from every other man she had ever known.

"I want to think about what you said and explore some of it with my therapist. I guess I've got some introspection coming my way. I think you're right, but if you're here, I'm going to get distracted. Give me a month, time to immerse myself in the idea that I deserve Goldie. I need to get there without someone pushing me. You got me started – now let me take those first steps."

She smiled at him like a summer breeze. He felt something in his abdomen tighten, and he showed his crooked teeth.

"I'll see you in a week."

"No, give me a month." Then softly, "Please?"

He'd won. He stood triumphantly. He leaned in and kissed the top of her head like she was a kid. When she did nothing, he stroked her cheek with the back of his hand. He didn't see her expression, but he felt her hand grip his so tightly; he was surprised that it felt like a vice as she moved his hand off her cheek and released it. She raised her head with a smile of such purity that he wanted to take her from The House of Rest and protect her. He knew he couldn't, so he raised her hand to his mouth. "Until I return."

She let him kiss the back of her hand and watched him walk away, then slumped in the chair. The smiling mask fell away. Fury, at his infiltration of her personal space and rights, flooded her. Her mind was like one of those puzzle mazes in a child's magazine, where you have to find the way out, but the route is not obvious. There were devious paths and missteps. She knew if she had a moment of rest, she could see the way. She had to slow down, and the path would become clear.

***

The man with his life etched on his face, who seemed immune to all her antics, rubbed at his eyes like a baby with the back of his fist. Her psychiatrist pulled in air through flared nostrils, and his mouth formed an upside-down boomerang. "You know you're making progress?"

She nodded.

"Often, when people are closest to breaking through, they want to run away. Is that what you're doing?"

"No. I signed myself in and can leave any time; that was the deal."

"It would be better if you stayed."

She felt like that time daddy brought home a diaphanous, glass bambi. It was so delicate, and she wanted it at once. But he made her wait. He sat her down and lectured her on its fragility and made her understand that even though it looked strong, a moment of inattention, of roughness, could splinter it - and then it could never be fixed. It was a responsibility she had to assume. There was pride and guilt when she finally held it in her palm aware of the power, afraid of it too. That's what the psychiatrist made her feel: pride and guilt. Pride at her progress, guilt at her request, for she had a secret desire to please him, and maybe if Christian hadn't threatened to return, she would have.

22

ONE MONTH LATER

Christian shook the rain from his umbrella. Despite the frosty temperature, he was warm at the idea of this journey he was about to undertake with Joey. At the reception, he unbuttoned his coat and blew on his hands until the woman behind the desk, with her hair scraped back in a bun, looked at him. "I'm here to see Joey Brinkley."

The woman frowned.

"She's expecting me," he asserted.

"One moment, sir." She checked the computer. Straightened up. "Sir, Miss Brinkley is no longer a patient here."

"What do you mean?"

"She checked herself out a month ago."

***

The first time her mother's boyfriend had made her touch him, she had held the Bambi daddy had given her in her hand and crushed it so it pierced her palm.

23

MOTHER

When Joey departed 'The House of Rest' and slipped into the deep leather seats of the limousine, she did not start layering on armor like she usually did in anticipation of seeing her mother. She had prepared for this conversation almost every day since she was fourteen. She'd kept the words geyser-ed inside, and this time, she knew she would not let them be deflected. She did not stare at the familiar scenery on the drive to Connecticut. It was only when the black bullet turned into the familiar driveway that she allowed herself to see the memories of her childhood – the good ones, the nanosecond of her innocence, when father was her hero and mother was the most beautiful woman on earth. Josaphina, draped on his neck in the pool like a clinging vine, mother laconic as Grace Kelly on the chaise lounge.

"Look at me, Mummy. Look at me."

Mother joining them, actually getting her hair wet.

"Mummy, Mummy."

Mother's face bronzed like a poster of what beauty is, her blonde hair slick, her eyes dancing, white teeth made brighter by the tan.

"Darling, you are the luckiest little girl in the entire world to have a daddy like this."

Picking her up and snuggling wet kisses on Joey as she squealed, then arcing up through the air to a shrill dolphin pitch, dripping perfect globules of water against an aqua sky above, hearing loving laughter below. A moment of pleasure and fear as she reached the zenith, out of mummy's arms, not yet in daddy's arms, both parents looking up, adoring their bon-bon of life. When daddy reached up, the forearms were sinewy and brown. Even though she didn't know the word yet, she now recognized it in her memory as virile. Being caught and carried down beneath the surface and knowing you were safe, in daddy's hands, with mummy there. Then back to the surface on daddy's chest, gasping for air, and mummy laughing concern, until she saw that her daughter understood that this was fun.

The cliches were in place. The crunch of tires on gravel. The statues arching around the driveway, the perfect lawn, the many ringed trees that cast dappled light, the stairs, the wrought iron door, and then the coolness of the entrance hall. And silence. The cloying silence of loneliness. Its stench clogged the air. Desperation had thrust itself on loneliness after father died, fermented with a lubricant of alcohol. She remembered the smell of fear. She felt it creep up her spine, creating knots in her neck, tightening her shoulders so the supermodel hunched, and the loping stride became a little girl stumble. She stopped and listened to the silence.

A house like this should be peppered with people laughing, sucking down life. It could have raised a granddaughter; it could have been a home alive with tricycles and bears, the paraphernalia of childhood. Joey closed her eyes, reminding herself that Goldie would not be playing with toys anymore; Goldie was now around the age that she had been when she was impregnated. She opened her mouth and let her full voice bounce off the surfaces with the word: *Mother!*

Unknowingly, she walked her little girl walk, tentative as a bruised puppy, toward the back of the house that overlooked the expanse of the pool, the lawn erect like a day-old growth of beard. Again, the memories crowded in, but she pushed them away and walked to the room that was all glass walls and seventies splendor. In the depth where the light from the windows did not penetrate lay mother. The air conditioner was on. The room cool, verging on cold. The constriction that Joey felt had nothing to do with temperature and everything to do with emotion; ragged, confused emotion that flushed through her at the sight of the woman who should have been her protector, who had imposed her brutal will - the wrong choice, *every time*.

This is where I learned it.

She recognized the trait that had become her own pattern.

Mother and daughter regarded each other over an expanse of mint carpet.

Mother had arranged the curved chair and ottoman so the view was in front of her. To the left, the grand piano, littered with silver framed photos of a time that was perfection in their minds, made more so by what had followed. Her blonde hair was scooped back in a French twist that was unraveling. Her upper lids were lined with Bridget Bardot black. Her mouth was colored coral with a matching arc on the martini glass in her hand. Her bony hands bearing rings that had grown too large for their emaciated claws were painted with the same coral on fingernails that had thickened and curved with age. Her crème-coffee silk pajamas made her look like she was playing dress-up in adult clothes. Her shrunken body, still elegant in repose, draped with regret. Her first action was to suck from the triangle in her grip. She jerked her glass to her lips, slopping the liquid so it splashed to the sunken curve of her breasts, where other splashes had dried and stained. Her eyes went to the evidence of a day elongating in the bottom of a glass, and she sought to hide the splatters with a splayed hand - that missed the location. Guilty eyes festered on her daughter, then flashed away to the garden scene, the free hand gating out in what had at one time been an elegant gesture but now served only to indicate how inebriated she was. She dropped her arm and reached for the whiskey bottle, filling the martini glass to the brim. She did so with great concentration and didn't spill a drop. With the task accomplished, she rested back, pleased at the proof of her control. Her head like a tulip bud, too heavy for the stalk, bobbing back toward Joey, bristling in defiance.

"Hello, mother." The words sounded like an inadequate script that a bad actress would deliver, forcing the director to chastise, coaching: *Unbelievable, try again.* She stepped forward. Joey, the wild woman, trying for politeness. "How are you?" The question seemed to confuse her mother. Her eyes fluttered around the room like a butterfly seeking rest, then settled on her daughter with a hopelessness that Joey recognized. "Have you eaten?" Off the nod. "Today?" Her mother flashed a sly look of pride that her daughter knew to ask the right question, and for a brief moment, the daughter was visible in the parent, then the mother looked away.

"I know why you're here. Your boyfriend was here before you, asking questions you should have asked."

The words were like a slap. The accusation was accurate, and Joey knew that she would go all the way this time. She needed to sit, so she moved to the uncomfortable functional chair that was the height of modernism circa 1972.

"*You* never asked." Her mother continued a conversation they had not started. "Not once. Then you send an elegant black man – with teeth that belong in Europe – to ask your questions for you. I did not reply. I failed to inform. I declared the subject verboten."

Triumphantly, her lip curled, and it struck Joey that actions that were sexy in the young were sad in the old.

"I never sent him."

"He said you had."

"He lied."

"A theme with you." She raised the glass and then moved her torso toward the rim, her coral shimmer reaching forward, chimpanzee-like, sucking a quarter of an inch of the whiskey. "Men lie to you, about you, and with you."

"Whereas they never lie with you at all. You had to pimp your daughter to get him to stay." Joey reverted to old habits despite her good intentions, and she disciplined herself quickly.

Her mother gave no reaction, and maybe she had not heard her.

Joey cleared her throat and spoke with the elocution of the northeastern United States. "I never sent him. I never asked him to come."

"Well, he came."

"He is not the reason I am here." It sounded awkward even to Joey. Old fashioned, like the statement should be followed by *thus*, or *sayeth*, but she found herself reverting to the formality that had been bred when she was a child, her defense, finally, control. "Mother, I am here to talk about Goldie." There, she said it. She felt like an ocean liner with a yawing hull, vulnerable.

"Goldie?" Barked her mother. "Goldie? It sounds like a fish."

"My daughter. The one you forced me to give away. I want to know where she is."

"Forced? Did I hold a gun to your head? Did I threaten to throw you out? You weren't competent. You chose to toss your daughter away, and then you chose to punish me for the act."

Joey thought she understood how Christ felt when the spear was thrust in his side when he thirsted and vinegar was given to him on a sponge. It wasn't the pain. It was the betrayal. *Do not argue the point. Get the information.*

Again, her mother smiled like she'd won.

"Where is my daughter?"

"Why has it taken you fourteen years to ask that question? If it had been my child, I would not have given her away. I would have fought to keep her."

"And let her boyfriend use her just to keep him?"

The woman in the chair who had born her froze in a stricken manner. She did not drink from her glass. She busied herself with depositing it on the ugly table to the side, away from Joey. She kept her back to Joey as she ignored what had been said. "I would have hunted her down if I wanted her, but you, you never uttered a word."

"Not after the first 5000 times or so. You're right. I failed to disobey you. I failed to fight in a way that mattered. I was fourteen. I will not fail now."

"I didn't know."

The words stopped the earth. Her mother had never addressed what had happened. Had acted as though it was immaculate conception, then when Joey's stomach bulged after her mother tried to kill the fetus, she alluded to Joey's indiscretion, her failure to protect herself, to anticipate. She fostered the concept that some boy had been allowed to do what her man-of-the-moment had forced upon her child, keeping the mother blameless all this time. *And now the excuse.* She looked over her shoulder at Joey like Ingres' 'Odalisque.'

"I didn't know."

"Okay."

"You don't believe me."

"It's not the point."

"It is to me."

"Mother, there was a morning that you came upon us in the kitchen on the verge of a repeated nightmare. You turned away, allowing a moment to be rearranged so that when you turned again, you saw what you wanted to see and not what was so clearly about to happen. You ignored hands dipping below pajama pants in what in any other house would be acknowledged as not the act of a caring adult but that of a man feeling a young girl in a way that was not normal. It was condoned."

"You could have said no."

"I did the first time. I repeated that word many times. And when I learned that the effect of 'no' was the same as 'yes,' I stopped saying it. When I understood that you knew and did nothing, there was no reason to say words that your eyes saw."

"I did not!"

"Goldie, mother. I'm here for Goldie."

Again, the mother and daughter fought a visual battle. Dominance, compliance, deception, and truth clashed like gladiators without a word until a reptilian pride half-masted the mother's eyes. "You've changed."

“Yes, I have.”

“About time.” The words would have, at one time, prompted a retort, and the clash would have been heated and long without a conclusion.

“Goldie.”

Her mother smiled, enjoying her moment of power. She raised the glass triangle and drained it, then lifted her left hand like an accuser. “In the safe. It’s all there.”

Joey felt joy and apprehension. “The combination?”

“It has not changed. Your birth date.”

24

CALIFORNIA

Everything led to California. Goldie. Fran. A chance to play 'Joey, super-model,' in a movie produced by Danny Stein. Opportunity. It all bubbled like a witch's brew, and Joey wished that she had not been chased out of The House of Rest by Christian. Joey had grown the strength to challenge her mother, but now that she knew where her daughter was, she did not have the courage to face her. She did not have the fortitude yet to say to her daughter: I am your mother. She empathized with Darth Vader. "Luke. I am your father." That had not turned out well.

The House of Rest had given her a glimmer of pillars to reach and tools to get there. But nothing she'd ever intentionally set out to do had worked. Not ever.

She did not have the confidence to find Fran, apologize, and say the words, "I love you." She still lacked the belief that she was enough. She could not look at herself in the mirror and say: The worst is behind, the best is ahead. If you love yourself, others will, too. She needed The House of Rest and the lessons she had finally been ready to learn but had not yet fully acquired, for Christian had found her there, and it was no longer a place of rest.

Just north of Sunset Boulevard, on Sweetzer Avenue, is a group of white stucco houses visible behind wrought iron gates. A pool the color of turquoise against dried bone glistened in the semi-shade below stairs angled to an expanse of Mexican tile that became her domicile. She bought a Karmann Ghia because she liked the way it looked and because it was a stick shift; everyone knew it had no power, but it was beautiful, she identified.

Joey painted. Her work had always been allegorical. Now she painted Goldie. Huge canvasses of round cheeks and blonde hair with the slightest of curls. Goldie had her mother's eyes, like glass broken, and refashioned as green pebble-art on a seashore. She had her father too. He had a dimple on his chin. The daughter bore the same imprint, like a stain in the dent below her mouth. When Joey first saw the photo of her daughter with the same indent as Joey's defiler, she felt the bile pump, so it blinded her to the little girl, and all she saw was her abuser. How could she love that? And in a breath, the answer came in a flood that wiped away accusations and recognized innocence. The girl was not her father. She was a victim – more so than Joey. Even though she didn't look the victim. Even though the laughter in her expression was so tangible, it threatened to bubble like a melody from the photo - the happiness was so dominant. Joey didn't trust photos. She knew that billboards across the world showed a confident, happy woman that girls everywhere aspired to be – and that, really, she was none of those things. Inside, she was the wound exposed, yet when 'they' saw the billboard, all 'they' saw was happiness.

Six weeks after arriving in Los Angeles, Joey drove over Laurel Canyon, turned left on Ventura Boulevard, through Studio City, and then south onto the oak-lined avenues that made up the suburb of Sherman Oaks. She located the address in her Thomas Guide and drove past the house without looking at it. She circled the block and cruised to a crawl, taking in the yellow house with the bright daisy bushes growing in diamond patches on the path. A huge Olive tree in front of a bay window. Iceberg roses on the property border. No signs of bikes, toys, or people. The sound of a blaring horn startled her. She was on the wrong side of the street and an on-coming car had slammed on breaks to avoid her. She corrected, and the Carmen Ghia sped off. She overtook twice on single-laned Beverly Glen, up to Mulholland, and took the curves like Jimmy Dean till she was caught in the burial pace of Laurel after three in the p.m. traffic. Then home and into the pool, shedding clothes as she went, knifing the turquoise liquid, skimming the bottom. Water above. Pressure everywhere. Her lungs were about to explode. *Goldie, a drive away.* She broke to the surface. All excuses had dissipated. Mother could no longer be blamed. An encounter had to be engineered. Would be. And she would be whole again. Surely?

The past decade had a nebulous feel to it. It was a journey and a trip, and it didn't seem to have an end; it didn't seem to be punctuated. Someone had once said to her, "You should realize how lucky you are." Can you only realize how lucky you are if you compare it to how unlucky another person is? A match has no light until it's lit in the dark. If you don't act in the moment, the flame burns out.

It wasn't an illusion. It wasn't an end. It had to be a beginning.

She had seen Goldie's house. Goldie wasn't just a dream anymore. But the step from tortured memory to happy ending was fraught with hairpin bends. Joey was scared. Grown-up was today. She couldn't justify deferment – not of responsibility, not of adulthood, not of accountability – not for a second more. She had to meet her daughter.

I'm so scared.

25

THE TRUTH ABOUT JOEY

Joey took a hit and checked her nose in her compact. Producer du jour, Danny Stein, 5'7, balding prematurely, was wired.

"We're here. C'mon baby, showtime!" Danny's Daddy had made a mint as a developer in the seventies. When Danny wanted to get into showbiz, Daddy stood security. Danny produced a little indie movie about holocaust survivors and their kids. Out-of-work-names who could no longer get arrested because they were past a certain demographic, signed on. Young, hungry beauties tired of playing the 'rich kid,' or 'the stupid rich kid,' or the 'cruel, beautiful, rich kid' almost paid to be in a movie where they got to be ugly and act the hell out of a role. Kids turned up to see their favorite television star and old people turned up to see their favorite has-been.

Ashes of Tomorrow became a hit. Danny's daddy made millions, and Danny was able to broker deals. *Face Now* was his second movie. He could have brought any of a hundred starlets to the premiere, but Joey was appearing naked on Calvin Klein billboards on Sunset. Every man in this town wanted to bang her. She was six feet, blonde, with breasts that stuck straight up, and she was all natural. He had only ever had silicone, except in high school, and not much then. The actresses that were considered beautiful were only beautiful by comparison to other actresses - who had their noses done, the best make-up, and the greatest light. Models were genetic freaks, and you didn't have to fight with them or their agents about money.

To meet Joey, he'd offered a walk-on role for her in his next film, a commercial project. He could always edit her out on the cutting room floor. Her agent had lubricated the allure of a possible career expansion for Joey with the proposal that Joey would attend today's premiere. Danny had jumped at the opportunity, but Joey'd demurred. Then surprise! A few hours before the launch of the film, there was a call to say she *would* attend. He'd quickly leveraged the opportunity, so they'd attend as a 'couple.' It was up to Joey how that played out. He was going to push it as far as he could.

"Ready?" he asked.

She hesitated. Danny leaned over and stuck his hand inside Joey's beaded halter. Joey was caught by surprise as the door opened and the paparazzi swarmed.

"You look so good, baby; show them what you've got." For a split second, it looked like Joey would revolt. "You got the part in the next movie – with dialogue. I confirmed it with your agent. The press release went out this afternoon."

Joey had said yes to the premiere to escape the old familiar anxiety that was having an orgy in her head. Home alone was dangerous. Solitude allowed her to cross-check everything she was not. If her time after Europe had proven anything, it was that her instincts were always off. What if she fucked up her daughter's life? What if Goldie hated Joey for giving her away? She'd die. She would. Joey would rather step off the world than be rejected by Goldie.

What if, what if, what if?

How do you know that the thing you intend to do will play out the way you want?

The thoughts had whirled without pause, and painting didn't make them cease. She'd needed something to interrupt her circular urge to self-harm. Joey had no experience with healthy love.

She had plenty of experience with sex. She knew sex wasn't love. It was nothing. She gave up her body as a sign of control. Hers. For those few moments, as she rode some man, she was in control, though they always thought that they were. She took what she wanted, when she wanted, as she wanted. They often sensed that she wasn't with them when she came, and it made them want her more. On a lonely day, sex was easier than masturbation. She didn't have to imagine. She'd disappear in a far-off place in her mind. Whatever guy was with her at that moment was her tool. She'd hold him down and ride him till she came. Sex was transactional. She needed relief; they wanted to claim her just to say that they had. She didn't care. They'd say they had had her even if they hadn't. So why not get hers? Leverage their ego? Her mind flew away in those moments as she disconnected, as though she'd never fucked them at all. No feelings involved. Men wanted her outsides; they never wanted her insides, and she never gave her insides away. Most recently, when she'd come close to gifting Giovanni with her secret places, he'd first taken them, then put her in The House of Rest. Better not to feel.

Dr Brand had told her she had to establish boundaries. Retrain her brain. Stop the cognitive distortions. That meant coming up with a whole new way of living. She wasn't sure she had the capacity right now. She was looking for easy. The mountains towered, and she had no grappling hooks to overcome their peaks on a new path. She was on the precipice sliding backwards, scraped raw by the speed of the fall. She was afraid to face her daughter. She was afraid to be alone in case she hurt herself. She was afraid she wasn't enough. She knew *love* wasn't enough. Love was untrustworthy.

HAMBURG:

Joey loved Fran. Sex with Fran was real. It had started over that painting called 'Man' on her first day at the Pension, when Fran had recognized her art. They'd find themselves in the communal room, talking into the night. Fran would ask: Are you okay? She would listen. When Joey and some guy had used each other for the night, it was Fran who'd shew him away.

Joey began going to Fran's room to talk. She'd sit on the chair in front of the mirror while Fran curled up in her bed. Then Joey'd moved to the floor at the bedside. Onto the foot of the bed. Joey ignored that this was what her defiler had done as he'd groomed her, had her confide in him as he gained her trust that entering her room was a safe thing to do.

But it was not her intention to seduce Fran. It was Fran who asked. "Aren't you cold? Do you want to get under the duvet?"

It was Fran who didn't move when their legs accidentally entangled. It was a slow tango of closeness and halts. It had not been manipulation. It had not been seduction. No one used anyone. There had been no leader, no victim. For the first time since Pedro, Joey had felt totally safe, and the time spanned as the women did girl things, innocent things, that kept Joey from running away from feelings and physical reactions she thought would never be paired. It just happened. One night. It happened. Soft strokes that turned into sighs, that became gasps, that had each quivering, so they arched and came and snuggled in wonder.

Because of her youth, she found it difficult to be physically close in a real way. Physicality triggered her. So, the miracle of Fran was that Joey could give and receive in a healthy way, unafraid. Not recalling her abuser. Not fighting her mother's man who would appear and insinuate himself whenever she tried to for healthy, safe intimacy. Usually, Joey offered up her body without a thought. Her mind shut down. With Fran, she felt everything, physically and mentally; her abuser stayed at bay, and she made love like a grand concerto, like the rise of a wave in a sun-drenched sunset. Like fireworks in the night sky. Uninhibited, uncensored. Safe.

CONNECTICUT: 1975

When she'd returned to Connecticut after giving birth, she'd had difficulty fitting in. She'd withdrawn. While her friends were connecting and experimenting with hooking up, the very idea of intimacy terrified her. And she was scared of what she might let slip about her time in South Carolina accidentally. So, she retreated inside herself. Her mind was consumed with her baby. Was she safe? Did she need Joey? Who was protecting Goldie? She didn't know how to begin to find the answers. When she tried for normalcy, and one of her former friends agreed to come over, Mother would hover, and when the friend left, the inquisition would begin.

"Did you tell her?"

"No. You told me not to tell anyone."

"That's right. No one would understand what you did."

"I didn't do anything."

"You did something."

Joey dug her toe into the mint carpet.

"Don't tell anyone, ever, Josaphina. Do you hear me?"

Joey was silent.

"Answer me."

"Is she okay?"

"I'm not answering you. This never happened. Stop asking."

"Mummy—"

"No."

"Please."

"This never happened, Josaphina. No one must ever know."

"But I know. I know what happened."

"You must pretend."

Joey looked at the elegant woman in her Perry Ellis lilac satin shirt, the shoulders emphasized, her long tanned legs in voluminous trousers.

"It's what I do." Joey's mother sipped from her water glass containing vodka. "I pretend."

"I can't. I think about her all the time."

"Don't." Her mother bit back. "Pretend. I pretend *all* the time. I pretend that your father never got himself killed and left me to raise you by myself. I pretend that…."

The child looked at her mother. Would she finally acknowledge what she'd allowed her man to do to her daughter? The mother turned away from her daughter. She presented her perfect profile to Joey, her free hand splayed across her chest, her fingers caressing her signature pearls.

"My advice to you, Josaphina, is to pretend. Just start. If you don't mention it, it never happened. If you don't share, no one will know. And Joey?" Her mother swiveled her head to look at the sprout in her school uniform scuffing up the carpet. Her mouth thinned. "Look at me, Josaphina."

Joey met the hooded gaze of the woman who was dressed a little too young for her age, making her look older.

"In my eyes."

Joey could feel the anxiety of what might be admitted ricochet inside her. "Yes, mother," she whispered, looking directly at her mother's eyes.

"If you ever ask again? I will pretend I never heard you." She raised her brows so Joey understood. "I will pretend you've never spoken. I will not reply."

***

When Giovanni had stopped responding to her, acting like she'd never spoken, ignoring her while she was right there talking to him, it at first didn't register that this wasn't normal. Joey had plenty of experience with speaking and not being heard.

26

CONNECTICUT 1976

It was a Puerto Rican on her swim team who saved Joey. He was the only Hispanic at the school. A scholarship kid the other kids shunned. He seemed not to mind. Joey wondered if he pretended too. Maybe everyone was pretending all the time? Maybe pretending was normal? Maybe it's what grown-ups did. Maybe feeling was abnormal? Maybe Mother was right.

It was a slow thing between her and Pedro. It began with him telling her to keep her elbow up on her pull to increase her swim speed. He offered to show her how. She declined. She got anxious when boys were interested. When they touched her, all she saw was her mother's man. Her heart would pound, and she'd either go passive and begin to hum like she had when mother's man had touched her, looking away at the old plush pink cuddly bear propped on the top shelf in the far corner of her room so she couldn't hear the things he whispered, and couldn't see his face; or she'd shove the boys away so hard they'd topple. She got the reputation for being a weirdo. She knew the name fit.

It was then that she decided she wouldn't feel. She would give them her body, but she wouldn't connect. It was like her mind escaped, disassociated. Her brain went someplace protected, like that moment in the pool between mummy and daddy, holding her breath beneath the water, safe, before being pulled up into the sharp light of the world. It got so Joey went from being the weirdo to being the popular girl with the boys. They all noticed that she hummed when they had sex, but - they got to have sex! Who cared if she hummed?

It was Pedro, with his lanky frame and brown skin that gleamed like glistening caramel when he hauled himself from the pool, who made no moves, that saved her. He'd give her hints to get her speed up to be more competitive on the swim team, and if she didn't speak, he'd nod, his lip curling into a lopsided smile, before diving back into the pool for more laps.

She kept waiting for the touch that never came. It was Joey who touched first. She was scared. Mother's man was right there with her, in her head, and she was ready to run. Her breathing shallow, Joey so intent to overcome, that she felt nothing but terror and determination. She tried not to hum. The pressure inside pounded, ready to turn feral when he touched her. She was at war with herself and the crowding memories because, with Pedro, she wanted to feel. That was new. She wanted to try normal. She was scared that if she felt, she would destroy the moment. As the volcano of flight and fight overcame the need to feel - Pedro pulled back. She realized she was heaving in anticipation, fiercely committed to the goal. Like a robot on a mission.

"It's okay," he said. "Slow down. We don't have to do anything. Just breathe."

That year, after she had given birth to Goldie, Joey established a pattern. She'd give herself away to some popular dude, be the life of the party, then scuttle away to Pedro. They'd climb over the school fence and swim in the night, talking softly, sometimes getting so close but stopping, always on the brink. Talking became her intimacy. Having someone listen. Not about that. Never about that. But someone to ask: Are you okay? And to wait for the answer.

When Pedro's family moved to Florida – the cold climes and subtle exclusion of their chosen home making them seek a less hostile environment – Joey was bereft. Daddy's death, the loss of innocence, Goldie. It all came gurgling up, but it also planted a seed she'd never considered.

Joey didn't have to stay in Connecticut!

Joey started sojourns into New York. Skipping school, she'd take the New Haven train to Grand Central and plot a way to reinvent herself, she thought maybe as an artist. When a man gave her a card and asked if she wanted to model, she'd said yes. When the agent advised her to go to Europe to get tear sheets - pages from magazines you put in a portfolio to show clients you could work - she'd agreed. She forged her mother's signature and applied for her passport by mail. The modeling agency fronted Joey the money for her ticket to Hamburg. When everything was set, she went to Bergdorf Goodman and bought the skimpiest outfits, like she saw in *Vogue*. She charged them to her mother's account, packed her suitcase in the changing room, dumped her school uniform in the trash, and hailed a cab to JFK.

Before she boarded, she called and left a message for mother. "Don't find me. If you do, I'll tell. If you think I won't, you're wrong. I will. Don't find me."

On the plane through the night, with the clouds looking like obstacles but proving porous to the plane, Joey created her new persona. If she gave herself away, no one could take her against her will. If she pretended, no one would know how she trembled inside at the things people did and said to her, at the courage it took to be the center of attention when she wanted to disappear. Giving herself away to be part of the popular crowd at school had taught her an important lesson. If you were in the spotlight, people saw what they wanted to see. The easiest way to be invisible was to be an image of desire. The price paid with her outsides. But her feelings were wrapped up tight in pretend control.

27

CHOICES

Joey looked at the horde of reporters fighting for her image as she was caught in the spotlight with the producer's hand on her breast. Her lips parted in a gasp of surprise. Her eyes wide open trying to comprehend what was happening. To the paparazzi, the expression read sexual.

Her mind whirred through her options. Should she cause a scene? Yell: HOW DARE YOU? Slap the producer's hand away. Get out of the limousine and tell the press that she had been violated?

Who would believe her? The way she was dressed? She was asking for it. That's what they'd say. And the image had already been captured. The photos would run. Plus, she was just a model without power. Models had no morals. Models had no feelings. Models were freaks who were paid to show everything. The more you showed, the more people looked, the more you were desired, the more you were paid.

She hovered in the open limousine door. Her arms gripping the sides of the door jamb. Danny's hand still on her breast. Her hair like liquid silver, her long legs wrapped at the ankles with sparkling ties that rode her calves. The cacophony of reporters elbowing each other for the 'shot' receded. She escaped into silence. She hummed.

Just breathe.

She heard Pedro's words. She closed her eyes. Danny's touch meant nothing. It was just some man touching her outsides, like they always did. She knew how to block that out. It wasn't real. It was an act, and acting was what was next for Joey. Every model hoped to slither onto the silver screen. This was what she had to do to get there. She knew her role too well. Smile. Flash. Crash.

You know how to do this. This is what they want. You don't need to be more. Joey – Superstaaaaar.

Joey recognized the tempting comfort of the old pattern she'd promised herself never to repeat. Pretend. Pretend it didn't touch her. Pretend it wasn't being done to her. Pretend this was her choice.

Joey smiled that supermodel smile. She would play the part. She would prove how good an actress she could be. As Joey got out of the car, she flashed everyone, top and bottom, her top falling away from her body, her micro mini riding up. For a split second, she had a déjà vu of the penthouse in New York, but she had no time to think. Danny laughed aloud with relief and delight, scrambling out behind her. Let the jocks who had shunned him at his private school on Mulholland see him now. He conducted interviews with Joey towering above him, her arm draped across his chest. Joey went on autopilot. He began each interview with a long, deep kiss and a grope while Joey stared sexily into the camera lens. If she got bored or he lingered too long, she would start to nibble his ear, slip a finger in his mouth while he was talking, work her way around to grab his face, and they would clinch while cameras rolled - and they would move on.

"Joey, over here!"

Joey kept her hand on Danny's shoulder and thrust her breasts heavenward, arching her back, slipping a knuckle into glossed lips, and biting down. The cameras created daylight in the constant glare of the flash. Actresses were sedate. They hated posing for the red carpet. You had to plead with their stuck-up-bitch-publicists for them to promote the movie they were all there for, but both the publicists and actresses acted like they were doing you a favor to talk to them, not the other way around. Now, here was a half-naked Barbie doll, arching and stretching for the photographers, attached to the ugliest man alive, but someone who was already reputed to be a player in the future. Joey slid naughty eyes across the press of reporters and stopped on a face that looked like it was on the wrong side of the velvet rope.

"Roma?" Joey recognized one of the models she started out with in Hamburg when they all lived in the Hotel Haben, where she'd first met Fran. She had called Roma that first day in Manhattan after Cannes, after The House of Rest, but the New York number had been disconnected. Now, here she was amongst the jackals of the press?

"Joey. Wasn't sure if you'd recognize me."

"Baby, c'mon here, walk with us." Joey pulled at Roma.

"Can't. I'm working."

"As a reporter?"

"Yeah."

"Man, that's like hustling on the wrong side." She grabbed Roma's wrist. "Come with us."

Other reporters turned and looked at Roma like she was a traitor.

"I'll catch you afterward, okay? I gotta work."

Roma's 5'10, all cheekbones and lips, with a body that didn't belong on the wrong side of the red carpet rope. Joey frowned. Roma was naughty, like Joey. She fucked people just for the fun of it, their brains and their bodies. But while Joey secretly did it to prove she didn't feel, Roma did it because she could. Why the hell had she settled for reporting about people in the spotlight when she could have been where Joey was - *in* the actual spotlight?

"Fuck work. Have fun," Joey challenged Roma.

Then, before Roma could demur, Joey used her full voice, not her whispery, brainless one. "Danny? Danny!"

Danny turned to Joey. He didn't like her urgent tone. Now she had his attention; she went back to bimbo mode.

"Danny, sweetie, look who's here – Roma!"

She said it like how Ed announced Johnny on the 'Tonight Show.'

Danny stared at Roma blankly. Should he know her? He'd like to, for sure. A carbon copy of Joey, but not strung out. She looked like –

well, a supermodel reporter? He looked back at Joey, trying to get a clue.

"Danny, make her come with us. You can do it. She wants to interview people. Boring-boring. Tell her how boring it is, Danny. You just spent how long being interviewed, isn't it boring?"

"She's right, it's boring."

"Not if I were the one asking the questions," Roma smiled, the smile she used from her days as a cover girl.

"I know, why don't you give her an exclusive then she can ditch the others and come have some fun with us? You'd like that, wouldn't you?" inserted Joey. She didn't want to lose the chance to reconnect with Roma.

Roma wasn't sure what Joey was promising on her behalf. "It's okay. You guys have fun. Nice meeting you, Danny." She took a breath, knowing what she was about to do. Taking the chance to get what she needed. "If you ever want to talk about the fact that every year we see a holocaust movie, and it gets nominated, and it's starting to feel a little like exploitation, you give me a call." She smiled a flat smile this time. His response could go either way. The next minute would tell.

"What did you say?"

"You heard me."

"You better get a clue," he fumed at her.

"Listen, it's not me. It's what's being said." She planted the lie and then baited the hook with what she really wanted. "I'd think with your grandfather's history and the pain of your people, you'd want to counter such statements. I'd like to give you that opportunity. That's all I'm saying. Not tonight, but sometime soon, maybe even interview your grandfather?"

If he said yes, she could sell the story to a national outlet. She'd scoop everyone. And she'd have the inside track with one of the fastest-rising producers in Hollywood. Thank God she'd done her research. The line about his dream project focusing on his grandfather's life was just a sentence in an article from three years ago. But she'd noted it. It was worth the risk. She held her breath, her expression neutral.

Danny looked at her, just like Joey, but different. This one had a brain. He appreciated her chutzpah, the way she hooked him with the inflammatory and then reeled him in once he focused on her. He had a script in development, and it was sure to be fast-tracked. It was loosely based on his grandfather's experience of moving to America with nothing and being chased and beaten up as a kid because of his religion. Dustin Hoffman was in talks to play his grandfather's father. Macaulay Culkin might play his grandfather as a very young child. Danny had seen him in *Baby Bach* at the New York Philharmonic. The kid could act even though he was only four or five. They'd have to dye his hair, but it could be a breakout role for him – if his parents didn't screw it up for him. All this flashed through his mind as he looked at Roma. How had she known? Research - or was it a lucky guess?

Joey reached over, grabbing Roma's arm. "C'mon, Roma. Make her join us, Danny. Promise her the interview so she can escape the press."

Danny liked the idea of teasing the story. He raised an arm, caught a studio publicist's eye, and then security, who hustled on over. Some words were whispered, and suddenly, Roma was over the velvet rope. She and Joey yelped like schoolgirls reuniting, hugged, and spoke over each other. Roma thought, I can pitch him my story, and Joey thought, Roma's close to Tara, and if Fran is in town, then she would have connected with Tara, so Roma equaled access to Fran.

At 4 am, the party was over. Roma had disappeared, but not before each promised to call the other. Most importantly, Joey had gotten Fran's number. Joey took in the crowd. The nobodies had left, and the wannabes had been shuttered out. This was now the inner sanctum. The party within the party - where the real power gathered. Still, it was the usual talk of who was doing what to whom. The name-dropping was thick. Joey figured people made a list of Alisters and strung them together in a sentence - and it didn't have to make sense. People paid attention like you were reading Voltaire or some other dead foreign guy.

She took another hit but couldn't get high. She wondered if the dulled effect was due to the new meds Dr Brand had given her on her second visit to The House of Rest. They could be blocking her high. Residue, even though she'd stopped taking her prescription? Dr Brand seemed to have the concoction of her meds right this time. No mind fog. Just that fear that she'd had since she'd seen Goldie's average home, reminding her that Joey's normal was another's abnormal. That realization had set her back and grown her doubt. The very *normalcy* of the house in Sherman Oaks threw her off kilter. It represented everything that Joey was not. Her fears that she'd expressed to Christian in The House of Rest ballooned. She would never be mother material. Had she fooled herself? Falsely believed in the impossible? The initial euphoria of seeing Goldie's house had given way to established coping patterns, old refrains: *Joey Fuck-up.*

Still, she'd tried to expunge the fear. Her sleep disruptions had returned so she'd used the sleeplessness to paint every version of the house with its diamond shaped, daisy-filled path, to remove the intimidation of that normalcy; it hadn't helped. Gradually she began to accept what she told herself: *This is me. I'm not capable of change.* Indeed, sitting there futilely painting Goldie's house, had made her feel like she might do self-harm rather than ever walk up that path and say the words: You are my child.

The call from The Agency asking one last time if she wanted to attend the premiere with Danny Stein was like a life raft. An interruptor. She could not be alone with her thoughts one more second. She was so scared. She was scared that she would never have the courage to face her daughter. She was scared that she was going back on all her intentions and the lessons she'd thought she'd learned in the House of Rest. Then the sobering thought: *If I keep taking hits to cover my fear, I might replicate the conditions that brought about the rape on the marble rooftop in New York.*

Giving yourself up was different than being taken.

She had said no.

That sick feeling of knowing that someone had owned her body without her permission, again, sobered her. It took her out of the whirl of never-good-enough to: *Never again.*

Joey was part of the crowd but removed. Suddenly, she was questioning her actions like she'd been taught in The House of Rest.

I shouldn't have done that hit. The warning clanged in her brain. *No more tonight.* She rubbed her nose and checked to see if there was any effect from the hit. Nothing. Her mind just got sharper, like an ice pick. Still, she needed distraction. She tried some random sentences.

"Michael Jackson is a freak. Jack Nicholson likes ugly girls and beautiful girls, but the girls he likes the best are the ones that look like bitches, act like whores, but have brains like a computer. Michael Douglas can act. Ralph doesn't just look like he likes men." She didn't wait for the conversation to stop; she just made her statements with utter conviction. The powerful people double blinked and looked at her, and saw how beautiful she was, and pretended that what she said made sense. Like you do with a child who has accidentally embarrassed themselves.

Joey also knew they treated her like that because she was on the arm of Danny. His movie would be huge, and she would have a cameo in his next commercial project - a piece had just broken in The Hollywood Reporter. His assistant had brought it to them around 1 am. MODEL MOVES TO MOVIE STAR. Fact. It was written in the headlines. It had to be true. Joey was going to be a staaaaaar. For sure. Well, maybe. And when she was a star and totally clean, she would have the courage to knock on the door of her daughter and introduce herself and make her child proud.

Be different. No more blow. Do it for Goldie.

The thought circled her brain. Maybe she needed to see that house in the valley one more time. Maybe seeing it would allow her to believe in possibilities, shake off her fears? She did not consider that it was the coke that spurred her newfound confidence. She knocked a line onto her collarbone and made Danny take the hit she wouldn't allow herself to take. She needed him wanting her, compliant, so he would do her the favor she was about to ask.

"I want to go to the Valley," she whispered while his head was close.

"Sure, babe," he said, not breaking stride as he snorted and continued talking to the fat guy, who even Joey recognized as heading up one of the large independents that were taking hold.

"Now," she said it hard, so he looked at her, but the expression wasn't pleasant.

She tried her little girl smile. Her old trick. Her one hand slipping beneath her plunging halter and the middle finger of the hand clutching the glass, outlining her lips, tonguing the tip like it was something else. His expression didn't change. She went to touch him, and he grabbed her wrist.

"Careful Bimbo. You think you get me hard? What he's saying gets me harder. We're talking power. You ain't got it. Don't overplay your role."

Whoa!? That was real.

Then her mind flashed: That was cruel. Maybe true, but—Deliberately demeaning.

That's how he sees you.

How to respond?

She twisted in his grip to get away and met the eyes of the fat guy. He was looking at her like she was a deli sandwich, and her decision formed, as it had in the limousine when Danny had grabbed her breast, and the photographers had already captured the image before she could react. She half fell into the fat guy, who laughed as his hand reached out to steady her. Danny was still holding her wrist as she leaned into the studio head, sliding her body against him, feeling him react.

"Want me?" she asked.

"What?" He laughed, unsure of what he'd heard, amused at the switch.

She took his pudgy hand and slid it beneath her top the way Danny had grabbed her breast in the limousine - almost like she was proving to Danny that it meant nothing. "Want this?" She laughed a seductive sound like a velvet night.

Don't do this. Don't go back to this.

"Don't be so serious." She deliberately pushed her finger playfully against his mouth, the way she'd done to Danny on the red carpet just an eye blink earlier in the night. She felt anger and shame rise inside but seemed unable to stop. "Smile." She instructed the big guy. "Danny doesn't mind. Do you, Danny?" She slid around, her legs apart, pushing her butt against the studio head but looking at Danny.

The producer was furious but couldn't show it. He'd called it; the fat guy was more powerful. Joey was stung by what Danny had said. He'd used her. She'd let herself be used. She should have left when he put his hand on her breast in the limousine, but part of her wanted to prove that having a stranger touch her body meant nothing. It did no damage. Especially if she was in control. It had been her mantra since the plane ride to Europe, where she'd reinvented herself. So, she'd draped herself on him on the red carpet, pushing it, proving to herself that this was her choice, that she had not been coerced into it. Now, here she was on the other side, having given him what he wanted, and rather than help her in her time of need, he expected her to wait quietly until he remembered her and then have her as notch on his belt. Dr Brand's counsel filled her head.

Walk away.

She knew she should have left when Danny grabbed her breast. She knew she should go at this very moment. Dr Brand had given her the tools to recognize that she could leave at any time, even if she'd gone to the extreme. She didn't need to stay in that place. She could walk away. But she had an intention. Something she couldn't do alone. So, she used what she knew worked.

Last time. She promised herself. *Even if sex didn't mean anything. Once more, then never again.*

She leaned back against the fat guy and looked at him over her shoulder, her lips brushing his skin as she whispered, "He said I'm your gift. Generous Danny." She smiled the smile that was on all the billboards and felt his pudgy hand grab her hip, holding her against him. She turned to Danny. "Let go now, Danny."

She smiled especially sweetly at him. She could feel his fury in the tightened grip. What was he going to do, though? Make a scene? Not over a throwaway model/actress/whatever. He released her wrist as though she burned. She gurgled back at him and stumbled away, leading the fat guy by the hand. Interrupting the discussion so important to Danny. No doubt the men would have it another time. But not at this moment – when Danny so clearly wanted it to happen.

She and the fat guy were about a yard away from Danny when she stopped and stepped back toward Danny, fast and sober, looking him in the eyes, hers clear and her expression serious. "That's power, Danny. And it ain't yours, not yet."

The fat guy came quickly in the back of the limo, then he made some calls as he watched her finger herself opposite him and pretend to come.

"I gotta get home," he said, ending the call.

"I want to go somewhere first."

"I can't be seen at a club with you."

"It's ok. It's not public. It's a secret. I'm not going psycho-bitch on you. I don't want to marry you. I just, can you do me a favor and let— I need to go somewhere."

"Where?"

"Sherman Oaks."

"No one goes to Sherman Oaks."

"I do." He looked at her.

“Please.”

“No.” He noticed the texture of need. “You say that like other girls beg for a role. What’s in Sherman Oaks?”

“Look, after tonight, I don’t want anything from you. You won’t see me. I just needed someone to be with me for something I have to do.”

He considered, then pressed a button in the leather recess of his seat and as the glass panel that separates the rich from the paid, disappeared; he instructed his driver, “Drop me at the house then take her where she wants to go.” He closed the panel and looked at her. “You won’t be alone, baby, he’ll be with you.”

It was past 5 in the morning, and the city was already alive, with worker bees scurrying to earn their dime. In LA, the dawn is unspectacular. Joey rested back against the plush seating. Why couldn’t she have eaten what Danny had said? Why did she have to act without thinking? Why did she have to humiliate him so there was never a chance he would forgive her? Had she made no progress?

Then, another thought. Those were the wrong questions to ask. Those were the questions that took her to The House of Rest. The idea that she should not disrupt abuse. Questioning herself on her right to say no. Mad at herself for standing up for herself when it displeased those who would use her.

Why had she let Danny grab her breast and not challenged him?

Why had she acted like that on the red carpet? Going to the extreme to prove it meant nothing?

Fucking Christian, chasing her from the House of Rest before she was fully whole.

Tonight was supposed to have been balm to her fear. But the emptiness of it had gotten to her. She was where everyone wanted to be, and it was nothing. It was a cracked egg discarded on a counter. Still fragile, still a work of art, but containing nothing of substance. Easy people to impress considering their level of success, brutal in the one-upmanship, and now that she had been made ‘aware’ in the

'House of Rest,' she found it impossible to maintain the vacuous Joey.

The scene was too reminiscent of the penthouse in New York, with the exception that she wasn't fucked up. She *had* recognized that she shouldn't take another hit, and that little admission had poked a hole in her fear. She *had* learned something. Joey would not be glitter left in the morning debris. She could face Goldie - surely? Maybe if she had someone else see where her daughter lived, her dream would be affirmed, like a talisman of the future she would create.

"Here, stop here." The limousine slid against the opposite sidewalk and stopped. It was late enough in the morning that people might be up and glance outside at the sleek vehicle hugging the curb. Joey chanced it. She got out in her bare feet. She crossed the road and stood in front of the house in the damp grass. Then she stepped toward the house. She walked up the path, past the overgrown daisy bushes, and halted at the front door. It was black inside. She peered through the window; the place looked clean and showed some style but was indistinct. She raised her hand as though to knock but stopped. Her balled fist opened, and she palmed the wood of the door and touched it so she could recall how it felt and know it was real. And in that second, she knew she could blow it if she was found at this time in this place. Her bare feet moved from the scratchy doormat that spelled, WELCOME! As she negotiated the excess of the daisy bushes, her hand broke off one yellow flower and cupped it.

The limousine crested Mulholland, to the land of the real people, Beverly Hills, but Joey didn't look at the mansions hugging the canyon. Instead, Joey looked at the absurd brightness of the daisy in a world of black and smiled. It was perky, spunky even. Not a flower one loved, but one that made you smile – and it was yellow – some might say gold. Her tapered fingers closed over the bloom. She laughed. She could do it. She would get clean. She lowered the partition and said firmly, "My daughter lives there. That is where my daughter lives."

"Yes, ma'am," came the reply, polite eyes in the rearview mirror, no expression. It was enough. Someone else knew. Someone else saw the house. It was no longer a secret.

Joey had a shoot at nine. Her mind wasn't on it. She felt wired. Maybe the coke had finally kicked in? Before Roma said goodbye, she had given Joey all the numbers of the girls from Hamburg, including Fran's. Joey fingered the paper. It was like nitroglycerin in her hand. The combination of Goldie and Fran in the span of twelve hours was like sex in public with someone you half cared about. She stopped at the thought. That was wrong. She never wanted out of control 'exposed' again. Sex in public? Never again. And if she ever found anyone to care about other than Fran? Well, she'd treat it as holy. She'd keep it sane.

Goldie. She didn't want to do something that would shame her daughter. She wanted to make Goldie proud. Joey had to try for Goldie. The idea of Goldie and how it could be if things went right made her happy in a different way than her hopes for a life with Fran. If Fran had the courage to admit what she felt for Joey, she and Fran could be good together. She moved to the big bay window where her easel was surrounded by paint, the drop cloth spattered and rough beneath her bare feet.

She touched the art paraphernalia and mixed colors. She should be getting ready. The light was losing its color to the dead illumination of a Los Angeles day. It sucked the life right out of the landscape and packaged it as skirmishes of intensity in rough anger on the freeway, in the ochre of a house, in the arrogance of a superior. The nothingness of the light always reminds you that in this city filled with stars, you were nothing, and even if you were on top, someone else had the secret to contort your achievement like a used tea bag. LA took color and replaced it with disconnect, as though something wicked lurked on your shoulder, eating up your moment that should be perfection and spitting it out in the judgment: just not enough.

She moved from the canvas. 'Now' was just not enough. She dialed the number.

"Hello?"

Joey closed her eyes as Fran's voice filled the silence. Her heart constricted.

"Hello?"

The static crackled.

The line went dead.

Joey hung up and moved to the midnight overstuffed love seat. She dialed again.

The call was answered quickly as if Fran had been waiting for it to ring again. Joey smiled. She could see Fran standing, looking at the phone, wondering. Going through the possibilities. And Joey's name *had* to come up. Fran had to consider that it might be Joey calling. She suppressed a laugh. Just like that, she had insinuated herself back in Fran's mind.

Fran didn't say 'hello' this time. She waited, and Joey waited. It was quiet between them, like a contest; Joey wouldn't lose. She held the phone against her shoulder, eased onto the couch, and touched herself. When the breath broke out in gasps she could no longer suppress and carried across the distance to Fran so that it was unmistakable - the quickening pace, the loss of control - the line went dead, and Joey came. When she opened her eyes, it was with happiness on her face and joy in her aura, languor and control fighting in the mix. Her eyes went to the clock on the wall, and she saw that somehow it was after ten and she was late for the shoot.

She remembered the feel of the door to her daughter's domicile beneath her palm. She paused. If now was not enough, when would it be? She needed to figure it out. She went to the unemptied garbage bin where she'd tossed her meds, retrieved the container, flipped it open, and took her pill.

28

GOLDIE - FIRST MEET

The mutt sniffed the air, its coat the color of a Beverly Hills socialite's highlights. Attached to the leash was an elegant hand and long forearm, unconscious in its beauty. Joey bit down on her knuckle.

That's Goldie.

There was no mistaking the elongated lines of the body not fully developed. It was how Joey looked in pictures before. The year she gave birth was not documented in stagnant moments to be looked at fondly later. No photos of a swaddled infant in the beaming mother's arms. It was as though two years of her life were zapped in an Alzheimer's moment that lived on a loop in her mind - a fantasy no one but her mother witnessed. Now, here was the product.

The blunt cut that her daughter sported matched the one the woman walking next to Goldie wore. *Her mother.* The vinegar image-saturated and cut, yet she could not look away. There was the woman who had raised her daughter - and she should be grateful - but she was not. Ferocious hate surged her being at the stolen time, the love that should have been hers, so clearly demonstrated as the woman softly, *obscenely*, reached up to stroke the girl's hair, the two laughing. *I should go to them. Introduce myself. Claim my child.* But she stayed where she was and watched the two stroll from her sight. The mother was stout, no make-up, short, the sprout next to her, willowy with youth. Joey stayed in her car until they reappeared like magic in the distance. Their bodies grew as they approached, talking animatedly, not noticing the beauty in the car, her magnate eyes absorbing the moment. They skipped up the daisy path and through the door that Joey had actually touched in the cool air of darkness, and they were gone.

There were moments in her life that were tattooed in her brain. The first moment, he touched her in that way. The birth. Her daughter in her arms. Daddy. Golden daddy. Fran. The miracle of someone who cared and was kind. That moment in the fornicating sheets. Hamburg. It was a happy time. Giovanni sucking away her sanity. That mind fuck that she was invisible. That life and laughter and happiness, the American dream, the American *right* - happened to others while she was stuck in a plastic bag, the air stale and almost gone. No one saw the suffocation. Joey locked in a perceived paradise. The anti-magnate. Unless you were a man, and then the eyes festered on you like a glutton to Almas caviar. That lascivious look that lingered on the breasts, the mouth, the secret places. That dank desire for parts to poke and penetrate, but that never saw the whole and didn't care what was said or felt. Shut up and smile, baby. Yeah, take it all, eat it, swallow, now get the fuck away. She was the discard of life. Once used, ignored, abandoned.

She was back in that mindset as she sat in the car in Sherman Oaks. She watched another woman touching her child. Strangers being intimate with the most delicate parts of her. The theme *déjà vu*-ed itself, like a chorus in her life. And then another forever moment flew away her retrospection of her life.

The door opened, and her daughter emerged alone.

A chance, she must take it.

Joey opened her car door and walked fast toward Goldie, her route direct and purposeful. The child did not notice, bent on retrieving the newspaper in the driveway. Joey stopped, unsure suddenly. She hesitated in the shadow of the huge Oleander tree, afraid to approach.

Not so the mutt who bounded after her daughter. It swished its way over to Joey, tail slapping the air, its license clinking against its collar so the girl looked over and called, "Boomer, stop!" Then looking directly at Joey. "She's okay. She won't hurt you."

Joey realized that her daughter thought she had stopped because she was afraid of the dog, rather than afraid of the moment. But the moment, like every moment you anticipate and hope for, had happened, and now it was past. Her daughter had acknowledged her, spoken to her, and that first moment was now forever.

"Here, boy." The girl clicked her tongue and patted her thigh, but Boomer seemed more interested in Joey – who still hadn't moved. Tucking the newspaper beneath her arm, Goldie pretended to be angry and in an imitation of an admonishment, gruffed, "Naughty boy, come here."

And. She. Approached.

She moved toward Joey. The dog jumped up, its front paws on Joey's abdomen. Joey needed to speak. This was the moment. Her daughter stopped within reach, her focus the dog. "I'm sorry. She usually listens. Boomer, down!"

Joey realized that the dog was the link. Dogs and men. They always sniffed around Joey. "Hey, boy." She scratched his ear in the special spot that makes a dog fall in love.

"Down!" commanded her daughter.

The dog sheepishly dropped to the ground, and Joey knelt right next to it. Joey had found a way in.

"Who's a good boy, then?" she asked, watching Goldie through her hair, the waterfall of platinum that matched the color of the blunt cut.

Innocent eyes looked at Joey, the dimple in the chin not so dominant in person, not so hateful to see the defiler's chin on her offspring, now that Joey had inured herself to the sight by staring at pictures and painting the visage before her.

The girl called to the dog, the wind blowing her straight hair like a flamenco dancer's skirt. She focused on her dog, but then her eyes reached Joey's. Recognition.

Joey panicked but straightened from her crouched position.

Goldie looked excited. "You're her."

Joey hid her confusion with model composure, a cover girl glance concealed the hope and fear. *Her daughter knew about her? Recognized her as 'mother'?* The wounds of the intervening years welled behind her eyes, threatened to leak. She blinked them away. Euphoria rose. Her mouth opened, and a laugh exploded. Joy. Truth at last. Confessions. "Yes. I'm her."

"The model on the billboards on Sunset? My friends will freak out! You're her."

Fan not daughter - stupid.

How do you stop a dam that has burst? A bomb that has been released? A bowling ball once thrown? You couldn't, yet that was what Joey had to do, there on the street in front of her daughter and the dog. The cork that had suppressed the pain and the love that had swirled together inside her since Goldie's birth, that had popped when her daughter had appeared to recognize Joey as her mother, had to be gathered up and contained, shoved back deep inside of her, so that this moment too, would not be soiled by the sin committed so long ago and which had shaped her every action. Joey fought for control and concealment of her state.

Goldie looked uncertain, aware of a blunder, awkward. "Are you?"

This is what a mother did, she made life easier for her offspring. Joey reached down and patted the dog's head again; her hair covered her face. She took the moment to gain composure, aware that her eyes were now level with her daughters. She raised hers, and there was Goldie, up close, inches away.

Joey nodded. "Yeah." She wanted to touch her daughter. But you cannot cradle a stranger to your breast and stroke their hair. Even she knew enough to know that. She straightened. "Joey." She stretched out her hand.

Her daughter clasped it. Joey tried not to react, but she wanted to write the moment in the sky in upper case letters for the world to see: *HER DAUGHTER CLASPED HER HAND.*

"God, I wish I had a camera. No one will believe me. I'm Jessica Phel."

Wrong name. She doesn't look like a Jessica Phel. Joey bit her lip. The girl, *her* girl was falling over herself. They were still clasping hands. Joey didn't interrupt. She watched the way Goldie – she will never be Jessica to Joey – the way Goldie's mouth took on the wide sweep Joey's father had when he was happy. She has her real father's dimple on her chin and her mother's eyes.

"You into modeling?" Maybe this is a way to penetrate further?

"No." Goldie laughed. "No, my mom would kill me. I want to do something good for people, you know. Maybe a lawyer. Change the world. Make it better." She grinned at Joey, then suddenly became aware that she might have insulted the model. "I mean, modeling is great, I'm sure. It's just not – for me." The girl looked down and realized that she and Joey were still holding hands. She laughed embarrassed. "Sorry." She extracted her hand.

Joey wanted to grab it back. *I'm your mother. You're mine.*

Goldie noted the expression of pain in the tall woman's eyes, aware that she caused it, but mistaking the genesis. "I mean modeling is great. It's one of the few professions where women are paid more than men. My mom says that, in a way, you can respect someone who – well." She searched for a compliment. "It's hard work." Self-conscious at having insulted Joey, she floundered for a way out. The door at the end of the daisy path opened, and the woman emerged. She looked at Joey. Joey looked at her. The fear mutual; the message visceral in both directions.

She's mine.

Joey did what she had always done.

Escape.

She spoke quickly and tried to make it sound casual, not urgent. "I've got to go."

"Wait, meet my mom."

The canker inside leaked into her eyes. Joey tried to make her mouth into a smile. "I can't. I'm late. Nice meeting you, Goldie."

"Jessica," her daughter corrected her.

"Right."

Joey turned. She didn't even pretend that she was headed somewhere. She could not walk toward some imagined place while the mother watched. Maybe her daughter wouldn't notice that she had not continued in the direction she had originally headed. She walked fast, and then she ran. Once in the car, she sped along Valley Vista to Coldwater. She drove through the stop signs. She sped on surface streets. A squirrel tried to race her. She slammed on the brakes. The squirrel, not so agile. She couldn't care. Maybe when she looked left, the squirrel had run to the right? She raised her foot from the break. Jammed it down on the clutch, ground the gears of the Karmann Ghia, and pushed down on the accelerator. The car skidded, corrected, and bolted forward. She did not look in the rearview mirror.

Since that first call to Fran, Joey had taken to calling Fran and updating her whenever she felt like it. If she told Fran, she knew it was real. Someone else was a witness to the secret Joey lived and no one saw. Usually, the machine picked up and Joey would download, like she had in Hamburg. She was surrounded by paints, a huge canvas on the floor, her hair pinned back. Her limbs splattered with the dark greens, blacks, and exploding yellows of the piece she was working on; she called it *Out of Black* – which is how she felt.

She'd purged her insides onto the canvas when she'd returned from the Valley. The painting was therapeutic. But now she was tired and needed human contact. Not a body rubbing against her. But the same feeling as when she returned to New York from The House of Rest. She was in need of someone who cared. As she had back then, she dialed Fran. She listened as Fran's voice delivered the efficient confirmation of the number and then asked for the name and number of the caller and a brief message.

"Hello Fran? It's Joey. Pick up." The static silence slipped by. Joey sighed and began to talk.

29

JOEY - THE MALL

Joey watched with refugee eyes feasting on her daughter. She was at Fashion Square Mall watching Goldie eat lunch in the food court with friends. She'd followed her and performed the action she practiced at home. Double take, surprise. "Hello!" She walked past the table of young girls, close enough that Goldie could see her. She did the double take, but Goldie was animatedly talking to her friends and didn't notice Joey, though an older Hispanic man did. He caught her eye and as she looped back a second time to try her practiced response again, he came over.

"Hey. You're that model, aren't you?"

Joey never knew what to say in these situations.

He didn't wait for a reply. "Man, my daughter loves you. She's got pictures of you all over her wall. She's going to flip out when she hears I saw you. Man, she won't believe me!" The guy is genuinely thrilled. Joey wanted the moment to be over. She felt exposed. Stopped like the lone tree in a field of shrubs in the food court of Fashion Square Mall in Sherman Oaks. There was nowhere to hide. Joey had a plan, but it was being interrupted. Usually, a fan wanted something, and it occurred to her to move the moment along.

"Would you like an autograph?"

"Serious? No way, man!" The guy was delighted. "My daughter will be so happy!"

Joey waited patiently for the guy to give her something to write with, surreptitiously watching Goldie. She looked happy. She laughed a lot, and when she did, she reminded Joey of the way her mother used to look before her father died.

"You got some paper?" asked the guy.

Why did people who wanted autographs never have paper? Then she recalled that *she* had offered to give him an autograph so she could get back to the task at hand - inserting herself into her daughter's life.

"Sure." She dug in her purse and pulled out an old receipt.

"Pen?" The guy patted his baggy jeans.

More digging in her bag. "No. Sorry."

"Man. Me neither." He looked around and settled on Goldie. No surprise, her natural beauty made her a standout in the crowd. He bounded the two steps over to her table before Joey could stop him. "You got a pen I can borrow?"

Joey was mortified. Goldie looked up, took in the situation, and smiled a big, welcoming smile at Joey.

"Sorry," Joey mouthed.

Goldie whipped out a pen from her crossbody purse. Joey automatically clocked that her daughter had style. She was dressed in simple denim jeans with a white tee and a small, red crossbody purse. Anyone else would've gone with a black purse. *My style* preened, Joey.

"Here." Goldie proffered a pen.

"Thanks, Goldie."

"No, it's Jessica."

"Oh, right. Sorry."

She signed the autograph, and the Hispanic guy took off. Joey lingered. "That was nice of you – thanks." She returned the pen, retrospectively grateful to the guy for engineering the contact.

"That must happen to you all the time?" Goldie's friend ventured.

"Sometimes."

"Hey, want to join us?" asked the third girl.

"I'm sure she has to be somewhere." Goldie offered her a way out.

"No. Sure. I'd love to join you."

30

FRAN

Joey's voice came on the answering machine as Fran worked. "Hi, Fran. I saw Goldie again today. I had lunch with her. I planned it like it was an accident, but I planned it all along. She's like sunlight, you know? Light and airy and none of the things she'd be if I'd raised her. I knew I shouldn't engineer it, but I want to spend time with her, get to know her, but not have to be her mother yet, y'know? I'm not there yet. I don't have my shit together. But I'm trying. I'm getting better at it." A pause. Then Joey's voice continued thoughtfully, "I don't know what to do. I thought just seeing her would be enough, but it isn't. Being with her is like a drug. No, better. Well, worse. Because the high is so good but the crash. Man, maybe my mother was right, and not knowing is better than knowing. I—"

The machine cut off.

Fran sat in her airy, sun-drenched home office, listening to Joey's voice. Waiting to see if she would call back as she usually did. Fran had pushed away from the computer when she'd first heard Joey speak, like she didn't want to be fenced in by the desk or the world or reality, while the voice that filled her dreams now filled her room.

Her clothing line had taken off and Christian had kept his word, marketing the 'IT' label like he had with 'Boot Shoot'. There was no doubt he was good at business – nor that her simple designs allowed women to be stylish without having to bankrupt themselves. In a very short time, the clothing found a niche market that was enormous – just like Fran had known it would. Since Christian already had the factories in place, it was easy to use the same facilities and staff for her patterns. The turn-around was fast, and they could barely keep up with demand. There was talk of expanding production.

Fran had kept an eye on Joey through Christian and then through 'The Agency,' casually asking about Joey as a potential model for her new label, just to confirm where Joey was.

If anyone else had called and gotten off on the phone, Fran would have been ruthless in blocking the calls, changing her number – anything to stop it. She knew it was Joey, though, and since that morning when she thought Joey was living on the streets, she'd admitted that what was between them was more complicated than friendship. It had crossed over in Hamburg, in the shadows and privacy of her room. Fran had opened herself with Joey in a way that she had been unable to do with anyone else. There was equal taking and giving. She came with Joey in a way she'd never done with a man. So, when Joey called and did what she did, it took Fran back to a time when she felt like she had it all – though she'd never admitted it then and was not about to fully admit it now.

Michael was gone; she hardly thought of him. She was surprised at how little she missed the man she'd planned to marry. But it wasn't that easy to banish Joey. Joey was impossible to ignore. There were huge billboards of her everywhere. She was on television as the mature face of Estra. There was also the guilt of Fran's last conversation with Joey. Fran had been cruel. She didn't know how to come back after the things she'd said to Joey. However, it appeared that Joey was not holding a grudge.

Fran filled her time with work. Luckily, there was plenty to do. There had been the prep to get her line into production. She'd had to meet with buyers to negotiate placement of the 'IT' label. There was the constant work of overseeing a production line, choosing fabric and colors for dye, and dealing with delays. Shipments. The workforce. The work was endless, and it left no time for self-exploration, especially the kind that Joey would require. Fran had successfully buried herself in work until the calls.

Fran moved to the floor-to-ceiling windows that looked out over the mobile art of California nature. Her Pacific Palisades house was high enough that she could see the delineation of the beach like an exclamation point to the continent stretching away up north to San Francisco and beyond. She let herself consider the Rubik's Cube of Joey.

Then, she factored in Christian. He wanted to rescue Joey, or more precisely, he wanted Joey. Maybe Joey would have a chance with someone like him? A good guy, straight up, but no pushover. He knew that he'd misplayed his hand when he crossed a boundary at The House of Rest. He pursued Joey obliquely now. Joey had an endorsement with Boot Shoot. Christian had stolen her away from Calvin Klein, and the new campaign would launch at Christmas. He paid a lot of money to make that happen, and Joey had only agreed to the contract after a clause had been added that at no time would she have to encounter the owners of Boot Shoot. Christian believed that he could turn that around. Fran was waiting to see what happened.

31

IT'S A WONDERFUL LIFE

Joey stood in the light of her bathroom mirror, removing her makeup from the *Vogue* Beauty Shoot. The shoot was part of the Estra contract. She'd posed for an inside spread with an in-depth interview. Joey landed the Christmas cover. They blew her hair into big fat curls and painted her face silver, with glitter sparkling from her cheekbones to her hair. Her eyelashes became enhanced with long fake white ones, and her lips plumped up with white lipstick and a thick gloss. The make-up artist touched up her glitter with a little lip-brush while Joey waited in a box of reflective light for the cover shoot to begin. She wore a white vinyl turtleneck with huge ruby drop earrings encrusted with diamonds. She looked alien and arousing with her silver face, ocean eyes, white-blonde hair, and ruby earrings. The image stopped you. The magazine would fly off the shelves.

The interview had been difficult. "What was your childhood like?"

"Like a David Hockney painting," Joey said the first lie that came into her head.

"What does that mean?"

The reporter wore tumbling black curls - natural or permed - and had one of those voluptuous bodies that were popular in the fifties. Oozing breasts, narrow waist, and a round bum that curved into full powerful thighs. She wore her curves with confidence, unashamed. Unbothered that society held up the Joey's of the world as womanly perfection. Carmen was sexy without trying, without complying with an impossible standard. She looked like Rita Hayworth in the classic film *Gilda*.

"You ever seen a David Hockney painting?" asked Joey.

"In books," replied the reporter.

"Well, like that," answered Joey.

"How do you feel about being the mature face of Estra?"

"Honored," lied Joey.

"Did it make you think about the future? What comes after modeling?"

"No."

"What will you do when modeling is done?"

"Whatever the fuck I want."

"Don't you do that already?"

"Yes. No. Maybe." There, she covered every possibility and provided the non-answer.

"What do you want to do that you can't do?" asked the reporter.

Tell you to fuck off. Be a mother to my daughter. Not have to reinvent myself.

Joey stood abruptly. "Pee. I want to pee, but I'm zipped into this onesie and need an assistant to get it off, so you'll have to excuse me. I'll be right back."

Between the next setup, the full-breasted woman asked, "Do you mind if we talk while they do your hair?"

"Yes, I do," replied Joey.

The hair and make-up people busied themselves with the task at hand, aware that it was typical to use this time to chat, but the star of the shoot didn't want it, and their responsibility was to Joey. However, Joey was just one model, Vogue and Estra were the clients. The magazine and the beauty house existed before Joey came to fame and would be there long after Joey was gone. Joey, for all her resurging notoriety could become one and done in an instant.

Milly, the tall, black Estra representative on the shoot, felt disaster looming. She intervened. "Joey, would you prefer to set up a separate time to do the interview?"

Joey turned to her with big, innocent eyes. Delivered her best Marilyn Monroe in a whispery query. "Do you think we could, Milly? I like to reserve all my energy for in front of the camera. Carmen is such a great interviewer. I want to give her great answers, but I feel like—" Joey pretended to search for the right word. "I feel like I'm letting her down." She blinked. "Maybe Carmen could write down her questions, and I can answer them later?"

Or never.

She raised her eyebrows as though the whole fate of the world rested in the reply, her mouth a perfect 'oh,' held slightly agape.

Or, more likely, 'The Agency' could write Joey's replies.

Joey didn't want to talk about her childhood, her failed marriage, or the fact that she was trying to acquaint herself with her daughter. And no, she had not given any thought to what would happen after modeling. Had the reporter thought about what would happen after she stopped reporting? Joey didn't think so. Why was it okay to ask people impertinent questions? Why did an interview mean someone could dig around in the parts one chose to keep hidden from the world?

Joey flashed her model smile, turning to the reporter. "Would that be okay with you, Carmen?"

"Of course," interjected the Estra representative before the reporter could reply.

"Maybe we can schedule some time when you're not shooting?" asked the reporter, seeing her interview detonate.

"Sure thing," rasped Joey agreeably. Not a chance, bitch. Joey smiled. "The Agency will set it up. They should never have agreed to the interview happening now in the middle of a shoot." She placed the blame squarely on 'The Agency.' It was their error. Joey was game, but it was just too sapping to do an interview and a shoot. "You understand, right?" She opened her eyes guilelessly, furrowed her brow, and placed a concerned hand on the reporter's forearm as though Carmen's understanding was the most important thing in the world to Joey. It was the same tactic Joey had used with Christian in the House of Rest. Sincere insincerity.

What could Carmen do but agree? When she had, Joey got up and threw her arms around the woman, giving her a tight hug. "Oh. Thank you for understanding." The hug was so spontaneous and filled with such warmth that cynical Carmen found herself falling under the spell of the supermodel and reassuring her that it was quite okay to quit the interview.

Joey tossed the last dirty tissue with the residue from the make-up of the Vogue shoot in the garbage and smiled at her win. For a second there, she'd thought she had pushed it too far. But the reporter had apologized for making her day harder and asked if she could stay and watch the rest of the shoot; would that be okay with Joey? Of course, it was. It was the least Joey could do.

People always thought models were stupid; it made getting what you wanted so much easier. Who would think that a model would be capable of outwitting anyone?

Joey let out a little laugh and hit the playback button on her message machine as she massaged moisturizer into her neck and face. Mother's voice rose like she was right next to Joey. "Josaphina?" It sounded like a bark. "Josaphina! It's mother. Answer." A sound like a slurp from a glass. Then, the voice continued with more confidence. "It's your birthday tomorrow. I'm calling now." Then, the real reason for the call. "Have you contacted your daughter? Have you considered that it might not be good for her if you do? Have you thought this through? Or are you acting like you did in the bed when she was born? Proposing ideas that are sure to fail? Josaphina? Do you hear me? Are you there?"

Joey stared at the machine; all traces of laughter gone. Her jaw jutted. She bounced a fingernail painted in silver sparkles on the counter as she reviewed the message in her mind. Mother. Mother being… mother. She quickly checked in with her emotions and felt shocked to discover that she was unmoved by the message.

She was not angry, nor was she fractured by her mother's words.

That was new.

She ran her fingers through her hair, massaging her scalp as though teasing the thought free from her brain. Then she laughed a laugh of surprised recognition. Was it possible? Had she finally reached the stage where her mother could not color Joey's perspective with her poison?

"Ha!" exclaimed Joey, brightening.

Quickly, she reviewed the last year. The dissolution of her marriage. The House of Rest. The weary man who she wanted so much to please but who wouldn't play pretend with her, who wouldn't be distracted by Joey's body. Instead, Dr Brand had found the right medication for her, so she wasn't suffocated in a fog but still in balance. He'd taught her what to do to replace the reactionary tools that always led her in the wrong direction. He'd provided emotional checks and balances to use as a guide so that she reinterpreted others' choices and came to sane conclusions. It was them. Not her. He had given her steps to practice. She had promised she would, and she had practiced them while she inhabited the little white room in The House of Rest. Unknowingly, she must have grasped them. She must have.

Maybe her quest to connect with Goldie had taken her away from her need to connect with anyone in any way. Maybe her tendency to offer herself on a platter for others to use or abuse, to give it to them before they took it from her, had finally ceased?

Had she evolved into an adult without any fireworks heralding that arrival? Without any of the pomp and circumstance that should announce that accomplishment? No cap and gown making the declaration to the world, nor to Joey herself, that she had finally graduated to a more sanguine human who believed….

What?

She followed the thought like a bowling ball targeted at a strike. What change had happened within that she had not registered? Had she reached the stage where she could evoke outcomes without self-destruction to herself or those around her?

The bowling ball of realization collided with the pins, which toppled like all the obstacles that had always hemmed her in. Did she finally have agency that produced positive outcomes? That didn't take her back into the cycle of extremes?

Could she be normal?

She recalled a promise she'd made to herself when she left New York. She entered the kitchen and scratched at the back of the cabinet for a box of herbal tea she'd purchased on her arrival in LA. She bought the tea that Fran liked to drink as a symbol of what she should attain, namely, restraint – like Fran possessed. She promised herself that she would drink the Nettle Bush Tea as a celebration when she was in control. The goal was to emulate Fran. Maybe Joey could be organized, sedate, controlled? Mother-material. It was a thought in a moment of a crisis that she had never felt she had attained and then forgot to pursue – until now.

Joey placed the box of tea on the counter with the same excited reverence others reserved for popping a bottle of champagne to celebrate.

Eagerly, she broke apart the cellophane and opened the container, revealing the neat line of tea bags. Part of her brain prompted a new thought. She paused, fingering the rough sachets of aromatic leaves. Could it be that she had never opened the box of tea because, on reflection, Joey knew that Fran wasn't really controlled at all? Could it be that something inside Joey had gestated since her second visit to The House of Rest and was coming up with deductions she had not fully examined?

Fran let her boyfriend manipulate her and lie to her. She climaxed on the end of Joey's tongue repeatedly on many trysts throughout their time modeling in Hamburg while pretending nothing happened between them once daylight dawned. Fran presented herself as Joey's protector to the world, and Joey played the victim/wild child. They both knew that Joey was the one who made Fran quiver and contract, squirming in the sheets. And afterward, they'd lie entwined on nights that were intimate beyond mere lovers but in the way of being in love.

But loving Joey made tidy, controlled Fran's life a mess. Fran cared what people thought. Fran had ruthlessly, carefully concocted her image. Control was important to Fran. She wanted the life society sold as the 'right life' to which to aspire towards. Joey's wildness attracted and repelled. Fran wanted Joey but wouldn't admit it. Loving Joey didn't fit Fran's image of 'right.'

Loving a woman was wrong, but loving a philanderer was right?

As the water boiled. A new thought occurred to her. Joey was more honest than Fran. Joey was more honest than her mother. The thing that drove Joey crazy was pretense. Pretense manifested in Joey by either clinging too tightly, like she had to Giovanni, in an effort to reach the truth, to be seen and acknowledged as worthy, or in acting like she was out of control, so she didn't have to face the disappointment of people never doing the right thing. Never placing Joey first. Fran was the only person who seemed to put Joey first, but her denial of what Joey really meant to Fran made Fran, in hindsight, like all the others.

Joey raised the teabag by its tab from the box and gently circled it above the cup, like the planets orbiting the sun. She followed the thought. All these satellites had helped shape Joey's worldview and impacted her cardboard cut-out of who she, who Josaphina Brinkley, actually was. To the world, she was everything. To the people she cared about, she was nothing.

The House of Rest helped Joey unpick her false narrative of who she was and why she did the things she did. The lessons acquired in The House of Rest had been learned but not understood.

After emerging from her second visit to The House of Rest that Christian had interrupted, Joey realized that she was doing just fine. Maybe not at first. Certainly, she had reverted to her old tricks at the premiere of 'Face Now,' but that was the last time that she could recall going to the edge. Yeah, she had acted out after talking to Goldie that first time, but who wouldn't? But even then, she realized proudly she hadn't self-damaged.

She plopped the tea bag into the cup and added hot water. Her painting helped her cope. It took the chaos and reinvented it as art on canvas. It calmed Joey. She reviewed the lessons of The House of Rest.

Part of her healing was understanding that maintaining the forced lie of what had happened with her mother's boyfriend had damaged Joey. It was okay to speak the truth. Pretending is what got her into trouble. Pretending that she wasn't in love with Fran. Pretending that they never made love. Pretending that she had never given birth. Pretending that her miscarriage had not changed her marriage to Giovanni and that she was not hurt and damaged by the people she loved most. Pretending that being the image that everyone wanted you to be at the cost of who you actually were was not as damaging as all the other pretends she pretended. All this in order to make others feel more comfortable while she squirmed in her own discomfort at the lies she lived.

But she was changing.

The tea seeped. She raised the teabag on the teaspoon. Wrapped the string around the bag as it rested in the bowl of the teaspoon, compressing the last water from the bag with its own string - the way the lies she lived for other people squeezed her sanity from her. That was a new thought. She rested the utensil attached to its depleted bag on the spoon rest and sipped, exploring the flavor. It was acrid. She spat it out.

This was not Joey. This was Fran. Joey didn't want a calming herbal tea. Joey wanted a hit of coffee. Fuck Fran. Fuck her mother. Fuck pretense. She didn't have to be more like Fran or more like anyone – but herself.

Joey knew who she was. She realized that the *Vogue* shoot had been another domino to her world of 'should.' She didn't want to answer questions she found too personal. So, she had stopped the interview. She wasn't going to do 'should' anymore. She was going to do exactly what was best for herself. No one was going to take anything from her ever again. She was worthy of better. She would not give herself away. She would demand that people treat her as she deserved to be treated, with dignity, with respect. Christian had been right about one thing. Joey deserved more.

Joey found herself breathing in fast, shallow breaths. She felt capable. It was a new feeling, like being at the top of the Eiffel Tower and looking over the edge and choosing not to jump. Anything was possible. She would figure out Goldie. Jessica! She corrected herself. She would figure out a way to approach the woman who raised Jessica and broker a relationship with their daughter. She didn't have to slither surreptitiously. She could create a relationship built on honesty.

She laughed again. Joey Brinkley was going to be fine. She did a little hip swirl barefoot in the kitchen. She raised her arms above her head and high-stepped it across the kitchen, Vegas-showgirl style, as she had high-stepped it down the white lines of Park Avenue that first night back in Manhattan after she'd called Fran. She continued the preening walk through the living room and stopped at the window that showed the blackness of the California night. She stopped at her reflection in the windowpane. A young woman dressed in fitted trousers and a snug black tee. Her blonde hair shimmering still, with sequins from the *Vogue* shoot. She looked fresh, healthy, beautiful. Joey reached over and touched her reflection in the glass. It didn't disintegrate. She whispered her truth to her alter ego, looking back at her.

I'm not crazy.

Tomorrow, she would turn 28. Tomorrow was fresh. She would start again, armed with the tools she learned in The House of Rest. In that second, she went from victim to survivor, and she knew, she just knew, that whatever the world threw at her, she would never disintegrate again.

THE END

Dear Reader,

I hope you enjoyed Damaged Beauty: Joey Superstar. I fell in love with this woman with a huge heart, who the world bruised repeatedly. I'm so proud of the way she evolved. My dream is that it will inspire women to talk about topics we all live, yet keep hidden.

Read a teaser below, from the next book in the series, *Damaged Beauty: The Corruption of Charlie Cross*. Charlie Cross is the 'Charlie' referred to in contentious conversations between Fran and Joey. She is a shadow in Joey Superstar, but takes center stage in book two. Their stories conclude in the third book *Damaged Beauty: Plastic Paradise.*

If you enjoyed *Damaged Beauty: Joey Superstar*, please leave a review on the platform where you purchased it or on my website: margaretgardiner.com

Add your name to my mailing list for updates about the new releases: margaretgardiner.com

Follow me on IG: margaret_gardiner
: @MargaretGardinerOfficial/
: @Margaretggg
https://www.tiktok.com/@margaretgardineruniverse
https://www.youtube.com/@MargaretGardinerUniverse

Sneak Peek

Damaged Beauty: The Corruption of Charlie Cross

Damaged Beauty: The Corruption of Charlie Cross
By Margaret Gardiner

Bony M throbbed, bodies moved, the strobe cutting the action into disjointed jumps, like a badly edited movie. Joey, Charlie, Roma, Tara and Fran were flowing on the floor. Safety in numbers. There's nothing like youth, freedom, and loud, loud music.

Joey was doing shots – fast. Fran, mother hen, was already moving in, trying to limit Joey's shot in-take as a Turk circled like a buzzard, Joey the fresh kill. When Joey got like this she was a beacon to every male with a hard-on. Never reticent in life, the shots removed the few inhibitions she had. Fran had her hand on Joey's wrist preventing her from taking the shot.

"Joey, stop. You're already wasted and you made me promise not to let it happen again."

Joey smiled like an exploding rocket, gyrating next to the bar, not giving up her shot. "Dance Fran. Don't you love it?"

"What?"

"If you listen right, the beat's like a heart in your hips. If you shut your brain down, they'll move by themselves." She put a long-fingered hand on Fran's hips. "Let them go, Fran."

"Joey."

"You're too uptight. C'mon, let it go."

Fran smiled despite herself. She gave a controlled wobble of her hips.

"Better than that." Joey turned from the bar, hips directed at Fran, weaving a figure 8. "Can you feel it?"

"Yeah, sure."

"No, really." Joey moved into Fran. "Let it go." She pushed her hips at Fran. "Follow me," she commanded.

Fran gave an awkward laugh, moving her hips. Joey turned her head back to the bar, quick as a bee-sting, and brought the shot glass to her lips and swallowed before Fran could stop her. She wiped her mouth with the back of her hand and gave a triumphant smile. Fran stopped moving.

"Joey!"

"Fran!" Joey mocked her friend.

They stared at each other. Fran unsure how to get through. Joey not caring. She moved her hips again against Fran.

"Don't stop. Keep going."

Fran didn't move, she didn't like being messed with.

Joey shrugged, scanned the immediate vicinity and her eyes stopped on the flushed face of Charlie.

"Hey, South Africa!" she yelled at Charlie. "Get over here."

"Leave her out of this."

Charlie came over like an eager puppy. Joey draped an elegant arm, straight, like a stick, across Charlie's shoulders, leaning in close, their foreheads touching. "Tell me, in Africa do they have drums?"

"Sure. I guess. Like any place. Or, you mean, cos it's Africa – or how?"

"Don't overthink it. Can you feel the music?"

Charlie looked at the wide, high cheek-bones, like the sand dunes on an African beach.

Joey was the opposite of Charlie. She was free, wild even. She never thought anything through. She acted first and made even the most gigantic problems seem cool. She had a string of Euro trash wining and dining her. Joey didn't care if he was a Baron or a pauper, she used them all openly and cleanly. Charlie wanted to be just like her – without the hangovers and the faceless boys waking up in her bed the next day. Joey was ice and heat combined. Charlie adored her and wished she had the courage to emulate her – though most of the time Joey didn't acknowledge that Charlie existed. Charlie was therefore doubly stoked to be there, in Joey's spotlight.

"Dance," instructed Joey, and Charlie moved her hips in the way the African women undulated, when doing their traditional dance.

Joey laughed, relishing her power. "Now the shoulders."

Charlie couldn't recall how the African women moved their shoulders. She frowned a little in concentration.

"Turn around," commanded Joey, and when Charlie did, Joey grabbed her across the torso up between her breasts, pressing Charlie's hips back, pulling the South African's body against hers so she could feel the movement.

When Fran said, "Charlie, stop."

Charlie ignored her. It was only once Charlie took on Joey's beat that the puppeteer moved away from her, mirroring her.

"On the bar!" yelled Joey.

"No!" said Fran. "You don't have to Charlie."

Charlie tossed her hair like a horse that'd been set free to gallop the planes untethered. She knew she didn't HAVE to. She WANTED to. She felt sexy dancing across from Joey, the wildcat heathen in any group. Charlie always felt wholesome. Well, not tonight. She hiked a long, faded-denim-clad leg on the bar, and pulled herself up.

"Hey!" shouted the bartender, rushing up.

"Back off!" spat Joey, through clenched teeth, leaning into his face, feline, ferocious.

He backed off from the surprise of her forcefulness. She pulled herself up, too. Looked out over the room and made eye contact with Roma; beckoned. Roma pulled Tara along. Resigned, the bartender cleared the bar of glasses. How could he complain? Management would've paid for girls half as beautiful as these to be up there, dancing. The four girls were giggling in a semi-choreographed spontaneity. People gathered, clapping, as the women shook their shoulders and bobbed their breasts, grooving to the rhythm, while Fran looked on, too controlled to give into the fun, but appreciating it anyway. When the music stopped the girls took different poses, like for a high fashion shoot. Frozen action captured and held for one full beat. Then while the others leaped off the bar, Joey went up on her toes like a stiletto shoed ballet dancer. She put her arms in the air, back of the wrists together, fingers splayed toward the heights. She was tall, but she stretched taller on the edge of the bar.

"Catch me!" she yelled, closed her eyes, twirled and fell backwards, a perfect 'l' - free falling through the air. The crowd pressed forward, as did Fran, and arms caught Joey, and carried her over their heads in the air – hands clutching and stroking, prodding and dipping, moving her onward like an esophagus in an ancient ritual, Fran one movement too late to reach Joey, until Joey was on the edge of the crowd, and slid down the body of the Turk.

Find out more: margaretgardiner.com

www.ingramcontent.com/pod-product-compliance
Ingram Content Group UK Ltd.
Pitfield, Milton Keynes, MK11 3LW, UK
UKHW032039030225
454636UK00005B/34

9 798991 751711